BURN

THE FIREFIGHTERS OF DARLING BAY 2

RACHAEL HERRON

Hga

Darling Bay Short Stories

A Darling Bay Christmas: Three Heartwarming Holiday Short
Stories

Honeymooning: A Cypress Hollow Yarn Short Story

Women's Fiction Novels

The Ones Who Matter Most

Splinters of Light

Pack Up the Moon

Memoir

A Life in Stitches: Knitting My Way Through Love, Loss, and
Laughter - Tenth Anniversary Edition

Unstuck: An Audacious Hunt for Home and Happiness

Nonfiction

Fast-Draft Your Memoir: Write Your Life Story in 45 Hours

Fast-Draft Your Memoir: The Workbook

Letters to New Authors: 29 Encouraging Letters to Your Inner
Writer

Thrillers (as R. H. Herron)

Stolen Things

Hush Little Baby

CONTENTS

Publisher's Note: This is a work of fiction. Names, characters, places, and incidents are a product of the author's imagination. Locales and public names are sometimes used for atmospheric purposes. Any resemblance to actual people, living or dead, or to businesses, companies, events, institutions, or locales is completely coincidental.

Burn / Rachael Herron. -- 2nd ed.

HGA Publishing

Copyright © 2014, Rachael Herron

ISBN:13: 978-1-940785-25-7

CHAPTER 1

The guy just wasn't getting it.

Lexie sighed and stepped on the pedal so her voice would carry to the firefighter who was on her last nerve. "2219 Ivy. Repeating. Two two one nine. Do you copy?"

Coin Keefe's voice filled her headset. "Copy two two one nine. There's still no one answering the door, and there's no key where you reported. Can you call back?"

"*Affirm.*" Lexie knew she sounded short, but good grief, the call was for an eighty-two-year old woman who had fallen in her bathroom. She'd told him that. What, did Coin expect that the patient would get up and go unlock the door because they couldn't find the key under the pink flamingo? Coin probably just wanted her to say pink flamingo on the radio again. Firefighters always got a kick out of the dumbest things.

Okay, maybe everyone at the fire department did. Last week she'd gotten to say that a person had slipped on a banana peel. In nine years of working dispatch, she'd never heard of that happening in real life. All the guys who tromped through dispatch to see if she'd really said what they thought they'd heard hadn't heard of it, either. *No one* slipped and fell on a banana peel unless there was a laugh track attached. The victim, thankfully, was mostly unharmed.

The woman's voice was weaker on the phone now. "Hello?"

"I'm still here, ma'am. We're trying to get in to help you, but the key's been removed from your hiding place."

"Oh, no. I remember now. My nephew borrowed the key the last time he came over. Oh, dear."

"Is there another way in?"

"Around the back, the sliding glass door should be unlocked."

It wasn't surprising. In Darling Bay, most people left their back doors unlocked, if not their front ones as well. Officially, Lexie disapproved of this, if asked for her dispatcher opinion. Of course it wasn't safe. Crime happened, even in their small coastal town. But heck, it sure made the fire department's job easier.

Depressing the foot pedal so the firefighters—but not the patient—could hear her, she said, "Engine One, the back slider should be open."

"Copy."

"Ma'am," Lexie said to the woman, "I'm just going to keep you on the phone until they get in there, okay? I want to make sure you're all right."

"Honey, I told you, I'm not hurt. I just can't move."

A lot of elderly people thought this, until they tried to stand. Lexie hated that she took so many broken hip calls. Once the first hip went, many people lost their mobility, then their strength and their resistance to infection . . . "I know, but just stay on the line with me a little longer, do you mind doing that for me?"

"Just one strong young man should do it."

Lexie smiled. "Okay."

"Or two. I'm not a little person anymore. Two strong young men should do the trick to get me back on my feet."

"I understand. I'm not that little, either."

"Nothing wrong with that, honey. Can you just make sure you're sending me the good ones?"

"The good men?"

"I mean the handsome ones. I don't want the old ones. Oh, and I want men. Strong young men."

"I picked up on that."

"Do you even *have* any women working there?"

What an embarrassing question to be asked on a recorded line. "We do. We have three." In the whole department, consisting of almost seventy firefighters, only three were women. Women belonged in dispatch, and always had. Not on the fire line. Or at least that's the way the fire department in Darling Bay worked. It was a thing. Lexie hated it, but it was a thing.

"I don't want any women. Waste of time when I need help."

"They're very strong women," said Lexie.

"I'm sure they are. But they're not what I want. Once I called 911 and all I got was a huge man who looked as if he drank too much and a couple of whippersnappers who seemed scared of me. You best not be sending me that group again."

Lexie was having a hard time not laughing out loud now. That must have been Murphy's crew. He'd captained Engine One before retiring a few years back, and he'd been the training captain so he always had the new guys with him. Murphy *had* liked his whiskey on his nights off. And his beer, and his ouzo, and his bourbon ...

"No, I made sure the handsome ones are coming, ma'am." It was true, actually. Tox was a big guy who struck women dumb as he walked past them while wearing his dark blue uniform. Lexie had seen it happen at Mabel's Cafe too many times to count. Coin, with his dark black hair and quiet confidence, was classically good-looking, Lexie supposed. Maybe almost movie-star good-looking. Reporters always liked to snap his picture, his face coated with soot, after fires. And Hank carried his height well and had a very sweet smile.

"Oh, good. Just the handsome strong young men. That's all I want." She made a content humming noise in Lexie's ear. Well, at least she wasn't the panicked type.

"They should be with you any minute. Do you hear them in the backyard yet?"

"I don't hear a thing, dearie. I can barely hear you."

Lexie pressed the foot-pedal. "Engine One, patient's still awaiting contact." That should get them to move a little faster.

There was a pause and then, over the radio, came a startled yip. Then Coin's voice, shouting. "Darling Fire, we're inside the residence. Get her to call off her dog!"

"Ma'am," said Lexie quickly. "Call your dog."

"What? I can't quite hear you."

Coin keyed up on the radio again but barking was the only thing that came across. Wild, frantic, angry barking.

"It's *really* important," said Lexie loudly, "that you *call off your dog.*"

"But I don't *have* a dog," wailed the woman. "Where are the strong young men?"

With a stomp, Lexie said on the radio, "Engine One, you're in the wrong house. Patient has no dog."

Tox came up on the radio, roaring over the barking, "Two two one nine?"

"Affirm," said Lexie crisply. "Ivy. Confirm you're on Ivy?"

A long pause.

Then Coin's voice came across the radio. "Darling Fire, we're on Oak. We copy Ivy. Switching locations."

Lexie flicked her mute switch so the woman wouldn't hear her sigh. Then she said, "Ma'am, those strong young men are almost with you. They're right around the corner, I promise."

CHAPTER 2

Of course it had to be Lexie on the radio. Coin thumped the side of the driver's door of the engine with his fist after parking in the bay at Station One. It *would* have to be her, when he was busy screwing up. Looking back on his almost ten year career, almost every time he'd messed up on a call, she'd been on shift to listen to him being a dumb-ass. That made sense—they'd always been on A shift together, and the dispatchers had the same 48-hour schedule as the firefighters did. Two days on, four days off. Not too shabby.

And that's why Lexie had heard him screw up. Again.

In the day room, he heard a chorus of laughter.

"Woof!" hollered Luke. "Grrrr."

Guy Mazanti threw a stuffed dog at him.

Coin caught it one handed. "Really? Did you guys go out and spend money on this?" How had the truck even found time? They must have left the station as soon as they heard the call, because sure enough, the little old lady had just been a pick-up-put-back. No need to take her to the hospital. They'd only been out of the station a grand total of maybe thirty minutes. Forty-five if you counted the time spent at the house on Oak trying to repair the damage they'd done. And the truck crew had time to buy a stuffed dog to throw at him. "Very resourceful." He tucked the dog under his arm and pushed the day room's swinging door.

"Hey!" yelled Luke. "We were going to give that to Methyl!"

Methyl was Tox's yellow mutt and spent A-shift days at the station. She had her own crate, full of the stuffed animals she loved. Methyl didn't need another one. The stuffed dog was Coin's now.

And it was time to face the music in dispatch.

Sure enough, Lexie was sitting at her terminal, head propped on her fist, her eyes wide. Those boisterous red curls were piled on her head and she had tired smudges under her eyes, and she was still the prettiest girl in town. "Hoo boy. I can't *wait* to hear this."

He held out the stuffed dog. "Arf."

She smiled then. Grinned, really. "Is that for me?"

"Sure is." Let the truck guys tell her later they'd bought it. He didn't have to come clean about that.

"Adorable. Now spill. How did you mess that one up so good?"

Coin sighed and sat in the guest chair at the small round table. Telling her about it was a good excuse to be in dispatch, not that he ever tried very hard to find one. Coin just knew he wanted to be near her way more than he wanted to hang out with the guys down the hall. She was round and curvy in all the right places, and that rose tattoo of hers wound so enticingly out from the sleeve of her uniform polo. How many times had he wanted to ask to see the whole thing? Yeah, being in dispatch was better than listening to Tox try to train Methyl to sit for the millionth time. "You remember that fire we had last year on Ivy?"

"Oh, it was the same hundred block, right?" She turned and punched some keys, her fingers flying. "Yeah, it was right next to door to the patient tonight."

"I worked the back of that on the Charlie side."

Her grin got wider. "So you were on Oak for the fire. Not on Ivy."

He nodded. "And then apparently I drove right back to Oak when I heard Ivy."

"And Tox and Hank didn't notice."

"They're just dumb."

"No, they're not," said Lexie.

They weren't. They just hadn't noticed. It was his fault—Coin was the engineer. The driver. Sure, Tox was his captain and he was supposed to navigate, but in a town like Darling Bay, with only twenty thousand residents, they mostly knew exactly where they were going. His guys trusted him.

"Was anyone home?"

"In the house we broke into? Yeah."

Lexie laughed. "More. Don't you dare stop there."

"We had to break the side kitchen window in order to reach the latch for the sliding glass door."

"Because it was locked, even though I'd told you it was open, and you weren't wasting any more time on what silly dispatch said."

"Mmm." Coin didn't want to agree, but she was right. "So we bust in. This huge dog, massive, maybe a German Shepherd mixed with Malamute, rushed us."

"What did you do?"

"I threw a sandwich at him."

Lexie shook her head as if she thought she'd heard him wrong. "A sandwich."

"Yep."

"What kind?"

"Peanut butter, pickle, and grape jelly."

"Number one, that is disgusting and probably illegal in seven states, and number two, why did you have that in your pocket?"

"Serena came by earlier with her mother, and she'd made it special for me."

"Because she hates her father, obviously."

Coin knew Lexie was joking, but it still struck a small, quiet nerve. Serena loved him as any eleven-year-old girl loved her father. How long would it be until he could no longer say that? Soon she'd be in her teens and she'd hate him just like the child-rearing books said she would. It would break his heart when that happened. "Probably."

Lexie looked chagrined. "Coin, I'm sorry. I was kidding."

He pushed a knuckle into the tabletop. "I know. I'm just trying to prep myself for the teen years. You know I hated my father. I don't want the same thing to happen with my daughter and me."

"I never hated my father when I was a teenager."

"No one ever hated Robert Tindall." Coin had admired the district chief, though he'd only worked under him a year when he'd died. The whole town had grieved, but no one more than Lexie. She'd been on the radio when it had happened. A hoarder's house fire on Smythe Lane. An electrical line had come down and draped itself over the chief's rig while he was taking over incident command, but he hadn't known it was there. When he'd touched the back door to set up his mobile radio post, he'd been electrocuted almost instantly. The guys had worked him harder than anyone they'd ever worked, abandoning the empty house and letting it burn to the ground, but they never got a rhythm back.

Lexie had dispatched it all, refusing to let anyone take her radio that night. She'd come close to not being able to come back.

But Lexie was tough. So tough. Coin had thought that night that she was braver than any of the guys on the line. Her voice hadn't even shaken.

Now she said, "I was too busy hating my mother," and her eyes sparkled. "Still am, as a matter of fact. More, please, about the call. And that disgusting sandwich."

"The sandwich is a joke between Serena and me. I told her one day I'd make her a peanut butter, pickle, and jelly sandwich, just joking around, but Serena latched on to it as a thing, and now she actually likes them that way. I don't love them—"

"Because you're sane."

"—but she thinks I do, so she wraps them up tight in plastic wrap and sticks them in the pockets of my work pants sometimes. I'd just found it on the way to the call."

Lexie shook her head. "How do you not find a sandwich? In your pocket?"

"Cargo pockets. Do you know how much crap we keep in here?"

"So you're telling me you threw the sandwich in your pocket at a German Shepherd. That's kind of adorable."

Coin felt his face go red. He hated it when that happened in front of Lexie. Nothing worse than a man who blushed.

CHAPTER 3

There was really nothing cuter than a man who blushed, Lexie decided.

Sweet Coin.

"Oh, my gosh, I'm tired of sitting." She hit the button that raised the bank of monitors—the radio, the phone, the CAD—so that she could stand and work at the same time. At least Darling Bay Fire had sprung for a new ComCen when they'd redone the station five years back. It was a small room, full of computers—six screens at each of the four terminals—but with the big window and the raised ceiling, it felt spacious enough. On the center table was a collection of colored gourds—Sue's contribution—and in an early nod to Halloween, a plastic skull lit up and blinked next to the fax machine.

Lexie finished adjusting her work desk to the right height and leaned against it. "Okay. So who was in the house?"

"A man who was busy ignoring his dog. He didn't know we'd broken in until we went back, after picking up our patient. He just thought the dog had been barking at squirrels."

"Big squirrels in uniform carrying sandwiches."

"He was pretty heated. We had to do the board-up for him."

"You should have thrown your pickle at *him*." Lexie bit her bottom lip to keep from giggling. "So did the little old lady approve of the crew I sent her?"

Coin shot her a sideways look. "What exactly did you say to her?"

"She wanted the handsome ones."

Coin flexed his right arm. "Well, what can I say?"

"I told her Engine Two was out of quarters, but that I could send you guys."

"Liar," said Coin. "It was a Zone One call. And Tox is way better looking than Devo."

Lexie crossed her legs under herself. "Devo is hot. But you're better looking."

Coin coughed, and then said, "Stop it."

"It's true." Lexie tilted her head, taking a good, close look at Coin. He really could be in movies, with that hair so black it was almost blue and those dark chocolate eyes. He had heavy cheekbones and deliberate eyebrows. His jaw was firm, and he kept himself clean shaven, even going so far as to shave at night sometimes. The things she knew about these guys. "Why is your nose crooked?"

Coin touched the bridge of his nose. "Ummm."

"No! Don't get shy!" Coin was so quiet around some of the other dispatchers they called him Ghost behind his back. They'd see him in the hallways, and then he'd be gone, as silently as he'd come. "You're not allowed to do that with me. We're friends. Besides, your nose gives you a ..."

"A ridiculous look?"

"A look of badness."

Shaking his head, Coin said, "No idea what you're talking about."

"Like you broke it in a bar fight or something. Like you did something that gave you a bad reputation."

"I can't believe you don't know how I did it."

How had she never asked? He was her best friend, the person she talked most to. Lexie leaned forward in eagerness, drawing herself closer to him by pulling her chair along her workspace tabletop. "Tell me you dropped your Harley at ninety on a blind curve at night. Maybe while you were outrunning the cops."

"Nope. Nothing that fast. In fact, I was standing still at the time."

"You warded off a robber who clocked you before you decked him, and then you returned the old lady's purse while blood ran down your chin."

Coin's eyes widened. "You're gory, huh?"

"I like to imagine things."

Rolling his chair a foot forward, Coin looked over his shoulder. In a lower voice, he said, "I was on a call. On the ladder, thirty feet up."

"This happened at work?" Why didn't she remember that?

"I was a rookie. I don't think you had started yet. Anyway, it was dark. It was storming. Lightning crashed overhead."

"Lightning and you were on a ladder? No bueno. Were you *hit*?"

"I was."

Lexie couldn't stop the little screech she gave. The business line rang and she made short order of it, transferring the citizen to the voice mail they wanted. Then she said, "Go on."

"Like I was saying, I was hit."

"You could have been *killed*. Lightning actually hit you?"

"Now, now," Coin spread his fingers wide. "Slow your ponies. I didn't say what hit me."

"You're killing me."

"I was hit by a falling branch."

Lexie blinked hard. "You were up in a tree?"

One nod. "I was. On a very important call."

"Cat in a tree. You broke your nose on a *cat in a tree call*? How is it even possible that I've never heard this before?"

"I pay the guys cash once a month not to bring it up."

Lexie laughed. "I almost believe you. Did you get the cat?"

"Nah. Branch hit me in the face, I stuck to the ladder like a burr, which your dad liked, when he heard about it."

"I bet he did. He liked stubborn."

"Once I was on the ground and bleeding everywhere, Tox told the lady who called that she and her kitten could stay up the tree till Christmas, and we weren't coming back."

"And now you hate cats, like every other man. Except you have a reason."

Coin rubbed his nose. "Truth?"

"Duh."

"I went back and got the kitten after I got off work. I climbed the tree and put it in my shirt and climbed down. Scratched my shirt to ribbons and I was bleeding when I put my feet on solid ground."

Lexie clapped her hands. "I am so mad that I've never heard this."

"No one knows that part. I don't even know why I'm telling you."

"Because you adore me." She knew she was Coin's favorite dispatcher, and he was by far her favorite firefighter, though she loved all her guys. "What did the woman say when you showed up with her kitten?"

He sighed, and the tops of his cheeks got that wind-burned look again. "Turned out it wasn't hers. She'd just heard it crying up there. She didn't even like cats."

"What did you do with it?"

He shrugged. "You know."

Lexie gasped. "You still have it." She waited for a second to read his face. "You *do*. Coin Keefe, that is the cutest story I've ever heard."

"Serena wanted a kitten."

"Do not *lie* to me. She's eleven. Your wife—"

"Ex-wife," Coin said.

"Your ex-wife was probably barely even pregnant back then. And don't tell me Janice wanted to keep it because I know her, too, don't forget. It's not like she's the warm and cuddly type."

"I will admit," Coin said, "that I wanted to keep the cat. So I did."

Lexie rested her chin on her fists again. "What did you name it?"

Coin sighed. "Nosey."

"Come on, tell me."

"That's its name."

"Oh!"

Coin rubbed his nose again self-consciously.

Lexie bent forward at the waist laughing. Sometimes

she was self-conscious about how loud her laugh was, but her big laugh always made Coin laugh, too, and this time was no exception.

"I'm sorry," she wheezed after she'd grabbed her breath back, "but that's seriously the best name. You are the cutest guy ever."

Coin groaned. "Great."

"Why do you say it like that? You're adorable."

"No firefighter wants to be adorable." He glared at Lexie, a dark, brooding glare that she didn't buy for a minute.

"That's how you get all the action, right?"

He goggled at her. "Are you kidding me?"

"You nag 'em with your adorability."

"I *wish* you would stop saying that."

"Why do girls go out with you, then?"

Coin stood. "This has been fun. I'm going to go see how Luke's getting on with dinner."

"Don't you go anywhere, Keefe." Lexie felt a stirring of excitement. "I'm suddenly intrigued by your recent dating history. Why don't you ever tell me about it? Sit."

"You don't tell me what to do." He said it with a small grin. They both knew she did tell him what to do. That was her job, after all.

"Sit? Please?" Niceness wouldn't hurt, she supposed. "I'll make some coffee for you."

"You make it too weak."

"I'll make it so that you can't stir it at all."

"Sounding better," he granted, hovering next to the chair he'd just vacated.

"So that the fork melts when you put it in the cup."

He sat. "Why would you put a fork in a cup of coffee?"

"You ask too many questions," said Lexie, filling the

small carafe at the water cooler. "I get to ask to the questions. I'm the dispatcher. I'm the one who grills you."

Coin raked his fingers through his dark hair. "I'm getting a little worried."

"You should be." She added five scoops of coffee instead of her normal two for the half-sized carafe and pushed start.

Engine Three radioed, "Three in quarters."

Lexie pushed the headset transmit button that was hooked at her hip. "Darling copies."

"It weirds me out when you do that," said Coin.

"What?"

"I can't hear anyone talking and then you respond."

She tapped the headset she kept on when she was in the ComCen. "I love the wireless."

"If it means you make me coffee while still working, I love it, too."

Lexie leaned again on her console and rubbed her hands together. "Okay. Tell me about the last girl you dated."

"You met her."

"No, I didn't." Lexie would remember. She popped a Tootsie Roll into her mouth. "Want one?"

He shook his head. "You did meet her. At the Christmas party."

"You didn't take anyone last year." Instead, Lexie remembered him dancing with all the dispatchers, one by one, while the other guys danced with their girlfriends and wives. He hadn't asked Lexie. She'd wondered if she just wasn't his type—maybe he liked the skinny ones.

Now was her time to find out.

"Monica," Coin said. "The vet assistant."

"Oh! The one you brought like three years ago?" That couldn't have been his last girlfriend.

He cast a look out the window behind her. "That's her."

Lexie spoke around the candy. "She was so *boring*."

"Really, Lex? Thanks."

She put a hand over her mouth. "Sorry. But she talked about her cat, like, the entire night."

"She and I had that in common. Cat-lovin'."

"See?" said Lexie triumphantly. "You're adorable."

Coin fixed her with a stare that suddenly made Lexie want to take back the word. He didn't look adorable. For one moment, Coin smoldered.

Lexie choked on her Tootsie Roll.

CHAPTER 4

Lexie managed to pull in a breath deep enough to cough. The Tootsie Roll dislodged from her esophagus.

"Do you need the Heimlich?" Coin was already next to her, his face serious.

She tried to laugh and ended up coughing harder. "No," she managed.

"Put your hands to your neck in the universal choking symbol if you do."

Lexie nodded. Sweat broke at her hairline. Was it the Tootsie Roll or him being so close that was making her so nervous? Her skin felt superheated, and she flipped on her desk fan.

Coin laid his hand on her back and rubbed firmly in a circle. "You all right?"

Had he ever touched her before, besides maybe a brief hug when they got together with the guys for poker? Lexie said, "Fine." She turned her chair so he wasn't touching her.

Time to take back the conversation. "What dating site are you on?" she squeaked.

"Losers-R-Us dot com."

"You're not on *any* dating sites?" That couldn't be true, could it? A guy like him would be swamped online. He'd have a hundred girls to choose from in twenty-four hours, even in a town as small as Darling Bay.

"Are you on one?"

She cleared her throat again. "Of course."

Coin stared at her. "You go on dates with total strangers."

"It's fun." That was her party line. Lexie tried very hard to believe it. She even succeeded some of the time.

"It's fun to go on blind dates and make small talk with people you have nothing in common with?"

Rescue Two gave an almost indecipherable squawk on the radio, but Lexie know Danny's mumbles well. "Copy," she said. "Rescue Two available on the air." Dating *could* be fun. Sometimes. In the last year, though, she'd only had a couple of okay dates with guys who turned out to be too boring to see twice. "People are fascinating."

"Tell me your most fascinating date."

She took a moment to think. "Last year, there was the guy who was a commercial fisherman."

"Why?"

"Why what?"

Coin's tone was pushy now. "Why was he fascinating?"

She'd been fascinated by his thick wrists. She'd stared at them all night, looking at the way the veins on the backs of his hands bulged, wondering if he was ... well-endowed everywhere. She hadn't found out, though. He'd called her, yeah. But she hadn't gone out with him after that one night.

But it hadn't only been his wrists that had fascinated her. "Because his job was so dangerous."

"Pulling salmon out of the ocean?"

She shot him the look that quieted most battalion chiefs. "It has a higher fatality rate than firefighting. Fishing as a profession has *the* highest fatality rate in America. By far." It was why she'd accepted his offer of a date.

"Oh." Coin looked nonplussed for a moment, then he recovered. "So you can meet amazing people online. Why are we talking about this again?"

Lexie twisted so she could reach her personal computer. "We're putting you online right now."

"That, my friend, would be a cold day in a very deep place I hope never to visit." He leaned back in his chair and laced his fingers behind his head.

Lexie lifted her phone. "Don't move."

"What?"

She snapped his picture. "And *that* is going to be your profile picture."

"What do I get out of this?"

Raising an eyebrow, Lexie said, "This is a conversation you usually have with a parent. But if you need me to explain it to you ..."

"Quit it," said Coin. "I mean it. I'm happy the way I am."

"Alone."

"I have Serena."

"Alone half the time."

"I call it single. Not alone."

"Coin, I'm single. Being single means going out with people. With friends. On dates. Doing things that are fun and frivolous and sometimes ridiculous and having a good time doing them."

He stood and got himself a cup of the coffee that had stopped sputtering into the carafe behind him.

"You don't do that," continued Lexie. "The nights you don't have Serena, what do you do?"

"Work overtime so I can keep paying Janice."

"And *that's* what I'm saying. Come on," she said, bringing up HoldMe.com. "Let me do this for you."

"So tell me," said Coin, leaning against the counter and taking a big sip of the coffee Lexie knew was probably still too hot. "What are you getting out of this?"

"Nothing but the pure, unadulterated joy of helping another human being."

"Screw that," he scoffed. "Not good enough."

"What would make it worth it for you? I'll write the ad for you, if you want."

"Nah," he said, taking another sip. "You'll have to do that anyway, since I know I'm not going to. Something else. Something better."

Lexie didn't know what he meant. "What else can I do to talk you into it?"

"A bet."

Lexie squinted at him. "I don't gamble."

"What about our poker games?"

She grinned. "That's not gambling. That's taking candy from babies. And besides, I don't trust you. What do you mean by bet?"

"A bet means we're both into this. That we're both invested. I have no interest in just being your entertainment, something for you to laugh at."

What if his feelings were hurt because she was trying to get him online? "You know I'm not teasing you. I'm pushing you because I care about you."

"Then prove it."

"How?"

"Put something on the line. Something that matters to you."

Something that mattered to Lexie? What *didn't* matter to her? Everything did. Coworkers' problems, and citizens' complaints. 911 calls mattered almost as much as the little old lady who needed help opening her garage door. Friendship mattered to Lexie. Family did, too, even though she tried to pretend sometimes she didn't have a mother.

Love mattered to Lexie. Since she and her last boyfriend—a tax accountant who had loved spending time with his online game more than he had with her—had broken up last year, though, she had tried not to think about that too hard.

"What?" Coin said, his voice demanding. "You thought of something."

"No ..."

"What?"

"It's too hard to ..."

"Just tell me."

Lexie felt her skin heating again. "Love."

"Love?" Coin's eyebrows flew upward. "From a website?"

"You asked what mattered," said Lexie, embarrassed. But she meant it. It was important. "Love matters."

"Love it is, then." Nodding emphatically, Coin said, "Love is our bet."

"How do you make a bet on love?"

He held up a finger. "One, we tell the truth. Promise?"

Lexie nodded once. Truth was easy. She often got in trouble for telling too much of it, and she didn't think she'd lied to Coin even once.

"And two, we *try* to fall in love."

Lexie rolled her chair a few inches closer to him. "How do we do that?" she asked.

"If I have to tell you how to fall in love, sugar ..." he drawled.

She caught his scent—not the normal Axe body wash that so many of the guys on the line preferred. He smelled clean, like he'd just taken a shower. Like soap and shampoo, and something darker, a little smoky. Old fire scents caught in his clothing, maybe? Lexie felt something jump in her stomach. "A challenge. Okay, then. You know I *do* like a challenge."

"Yep," he said. "The last person to fall in love has to ..."

"Buy they other person dinner," said Lexie triumphantly.

"Are you serious? We're talking about changing our lives permanently, drawing other people into this game, and you think buying dinner will do it? No way. Go bigger."

"True," she said. "Okay. Bigger. Okay, the second person to fall in love has to buy the first one ... an *expensive* dinner for two, for the winner and his or her new squeeze. At La Spezia."

Coin groaned. "Bigger. What about a trip?"

"Ooh!" This was something she could get behind. "Where? Reno? Tahoe?"

"Hawaii."

Lexie was impressed but didn't want to show it. "Why stop there? Why not Tahiti? Or ..." She brought up the website she'd been looking at earlier. "Check this out. Bora Bora."

The picture she showed him was of idyllic thatched roof huts, staggered along joined piers. Each hut sat above crystal blue water. It looked like Lexie thought heaven should, if she got to talk to God about it.

"That." Coin pointed at the screen. "If you fall in love first, I'll buy you and your guy two round-trip tickets to Bora Bora."

"But that's so expensive!"

"What?" he said. "This is your idea. Besides, you're single, no kids, and you work overtime, just like me. You have the money."

What would have sounded rude anywhere else just came out as blunt. It was true. Most of them in the department worked too much, and money just kind of stacked up in the bank. Lexie wasn't great at spending it on herself, so her savings got bigger every year. Definitely a perk of the job.

Lexie narrowed her eyes. "But do *you* want to go to Bora Bora? Really? Because I can see you throwing the whole bet just to prove your point. You'll let me fall in love, and then send me and my ridiculously cute boyfriend away to the islands."

"You think I'm that generous?"

"Yes." One year, Lexie had run the Adopt-a-Family for Christmas, an annual tradition at the fire house. For one needy family the entire department had raised almost seven thousand dollars' worth of gifts. Then Coin's money had come in. He'd tried to make it anonymous, but the computer transaction had let his name slip through. He'd more than doubled the amount raised, and the family had been able to buy a used van with his funds. Lexie was the only one who knew. She hadn't run the program in subsequent years, but every year, she knew that something similar happened, moneywise. She had her suspicions.

"And what am I supposed to do if *I* win? Take Serena with me on the days I'm supposed to have her? Janice never lets me get out of a single one of my days."

"Have you ever, even once, *wanted* to get out of a day with your daughter?"

Coin had the grace to look chagrined. "No. But I know if I did, Janice would throw a fit and say she had an out-of-town business trip or something.

"I'll babysit, then."

"You?"

"Hey! What's wrong with me? I find your surprise offensive, my friend. And Serena's my little pal."

Coin drained his coffee cup and thumped it on the table. "When was the last time you babysat?"

Lexie stuck out her tongue at him.

"When?"

"I am a superb babysitter. I got an award for it once."

"How old were you?"

She'd been thirteen, and it had been an automatic award, given by 4H for completing the babysitting class. "Old enough."

"So you haven't watched a kid since you were a teenager." Coin grabbed a mug from under the microwave and poured her a cup. Without asking, he added cream.

"Thank you. How do you always know what I need?"

"Just because you're too stubborn to ask for anyone's help doesn't mean I can't read you like a book," said Coin.

"Hey, by the way, if she chokes on anything, I'm shockingly familiar with how to dial 911."

"Is that supposed to make me feel better?"

"What if I tell you I give CPR instructions all the time?"

"I am never, ever leaving my kid alone with you."

Lexie grinned. "Seriously. We could do this."

"Fall in love?"

For one long moment, Coin's dark gaze met hers. He

held her eyes for one second too long, and Lexie felt that strange thump echoing in the pit of her stomach again.

"Yeah. We could." Then she clarified, "Find someone to love. We could do that."

"Why don't you just go out with me, and we can cut out the middle part?"

She stared at him.

Then she laughed. "Oh, cut it out. For a second I thought you were serious."

There was a pause before he laughed, too. "A race to love," he said. "This is the most stupid plan we've ever come up with."

Lexie felt that hollow thump again and decided she was just hungry. "Agreed," she said. "Now. What's your profile name going to be?"

CHAPTER 5

"I want peanut butter, pickles, and grape jelly," Serena said without looking up from her book. "Extra pickles." She sat at the kitchen table, her legs twisted, pretzel-like, under the chair. One hand twirled a dirty-blond strand of hair while her other hand tapped the table next to her Harry Potter book. Always in motion, always moving. And always reading. At least she got that from him. To both Coin and his daughter, the perfect evening was pizza night with books. Total silence, except for the sound of crunching and pages flipping.

"Color me surprised," said Coin. He made the sandwich, cutting off the crusts without being asked.

"Thanks," she said, taking it without lifting her eyes from the page.

"How many times have you read that one?"

She looked surprised, and turned the book over to look at the cover. "*The Philosopher's Stone?* Maybe only eight or nine times. I haven't reread it as much as the other ones."

"Why not?"

"It was under the bed for a while."

"That'll do it."

Serena had inherited her mother's acceptance of chaos. Coin sometimes literally walked behind Serena, catching things as she dropped them to the floor. A book, an umbrella, her jacket, two more books, a comic, a comb, a lip gloss. She scattered things like a dog shaking water off its back.

He didn't mind. He hadn't liked tidying up after his ex-wife who should have been old enough to know better, but his daughter? Coin would happily clean up after her until she was sixty without minding a bit. He knew that.

Coin made himself a sandwich, carefully omitting the pickles, sticking to PB&J.

Serena didn't look up when he sat. She wiped her hand absentmindedly on her jeans. The smear of jelly matched a couple of other smears that she must have picked up earlier in her day at school. He studied the color.

"Ketchup? Did you have tater tots at school today?"

"Sweet potato tots. Yeah." Serena turned a page and took another large bite of sandwich.

"I don't even know what that means. What's that?"

Serena groaned, and inwardly, so did Coin. His daughter was only eleven. Okay, almost twelve. How did she already know how to make that disgusted teenaged sound?

"Dad. It's sweet potatoes. In tot form."

He felt gratified that she'd looked up at him. "Sounds great to me."

"Yeah." Her eyes dropped again to the book.

"Hey. Before you go back to that?"

With a barely suppressed sigh, Serena said again, "Yeah?"

Coin didn't have a way to say it smoothly. Just better to

say it, ignoring the nerves that danced in his stomach. "I was talking to my friend at work yesterday. You know her, Lexie? In dispatch?"

"Duh. Yeah. Is she getting a new tattoo?"

"I have no idea." For a moment, Coin was distracted by thinking about the way the roses wound out the sleeve of Lexie's work shirt.

"Are *you* getting a tattoo?"

"Not anytime soon."

"You should. When can I get my first tattoo?"

"When you catch up to my age." What he meant was when he was dead and in his grave and even then he'd probably roll over, but if he said that, she'd probably be the first sixth grader to get an illegal tattoo in Darling Bay. Heck, she was good enough with the computer that she could probably figure out how to give herself one, safety pin and pen ink, prison style. And his daughter was enough of a badass that she could probably do it.

"That's not fair. I'll never catch up to you."

"When we're older, time slows down. And it speeds up for you. By the time you're sixty, you will have caught up with your old man."

An eye-roll. "So what were you going to say about Lexie? Are you two dating or something?"

The question caught Coin flat footed. "Why do you ask that?"

Serena just stared at him. She had a smudge of black under her right eye. Coin reached out and tried to wipe it off. "What is this? You look like someone punched you."

She perked up. "Really? Does it look like a black eye?"

"No. Like you were trying on mascara or something."

Serena deflated, poking a finger at the remaining half of her sandwich.

Coin felt he barely had control of this conversation, something he felt more and more often these days. "You were trying on mascara?"

"Sophie made me. But then she stuck the wand in her eye and then her mom had to wash it out and she cried for like half an hour." She scrubbed at her eye with the back of her hand.

"You're only making it worse. Cut that out." Coin got up and wetted a piece of paper towel. He held her chin still and rubbed under her eye with his other hand. "What is this stuff made out of? Tar?"

"Quit it, I'll get it off in the bath. So, you and Lexie are dating?"

"No, we're not."

"Okay. I didn't think so, anyway."

"Why not?"

"Dad."

"What?"

"You're kind of ..."

"What?" Now Coin really wanted to know.

"You're kind of not that cool."

"You're my kid," Coin said as easily as he could. It still stung a bit. Strangely. "You're supposed to be embarrassed of me."

Serena shook her head. "I'm not embarrassed. You're a fireman. That gives you automatic cred."

Cred?

She went on, "But you're not exactly outgoing enough for her."

"You sound like you're twenty. You scare me."

"What can I say? I'm mature for my age. Can I have a tattoo when I'm sixteen?"

"No. What if I dated someone else?"

"Who?"

"No one you know."

"Who?" Serena didn't even look bothered. She looked genuinely interested.

"Someone online."

"*You're* going to do online dating?"

"Oh, come on, Serena. Like I'm the very last one in the whole world who would go on the internet to find a date."

She raised one eyebrow archly. She looked like Janice when she did that. Pretty. And calculating. "I think you are. There's that guy you work with, the one I call Lurch?"

"Devo."

"He would be the last. But you would be the second-to-last."

"So I'm right at the back of the pack with a guy who eats rocks for breakfast."

In front of his eyes, she changed back into a little girl, all giggles. "He does not."

"I've seen it. Rocks. Like cereal, but rocky."

Delightedly, she said, "Gross!"

"He pours sand on top, instead of sugar."

"What does he use for milk?"

Coin leaned forward and whispered, "Tide pool water. The scummy kind, where it's been sitting for days in the sun. He likes it warm."

Serena almost fell off her chair laughing.

When she'd calmed a bit and had finished her sandwich, he said, "So you wouldn't mind? If I dated?"

"You don't want to just date Mom?" she asked hopefully.

"Baby. You know she's happy with Tom. And you like him, too."

A shrug was his only answer.

They'd been clear when they'd separated five years ago. It had been as amicable as a woman leaving one man for another ever could be. "And I'm happy, too."

"Then why do you want to change that?"

Coin thought. "You ask good questions, you know that?"

She nodded. "Yes."

"I don't know the answer to that." For a moment, Lexie's big brown eyes and messy red curls flashed in front of him. "Because it's time, I think."

"Fine," she said, lowering her head to her book again.

"Serena."

"Really, Dad." She reached out and patted the back of his hand without looking up. "It's fine by me. This time, though, try to date someone who likes sports. Mom does *not* like sports."

"Neither do I," said Coin. "You still like me."

Another long-suffering sigh. "If someone doesn't teach me how to throw a softball and soon, I'm not even going to make the team."

"Sorry, slugger."

"It's okay. Now shush. I'm reading."

CHAPTER 6

Lexie's brother James was already on the couch when she let herself into her mother's house.

"You're late."

"I am not," said Lexie, glancing at a non-existent watch on her right wrist. "I'm perfectly on time."

The only way Lexie ever got out of Friday night dinner was by being at work—where her mother usually called her at least once to make sure she wasn't lying, which was actually fair, since she *would* lie about it if she'd been able to get away with it—or if she was dead. So far the dead part hadn't happened, and because she worked two out of every six days and her days off rotated, she had to have dinner four out of every six Fridays.

She was better off than James, of course. Her older brother had to eat every single Friday night there.

"You're five minutes late, so I'm leaving five minutes before you," he said.

"Always right down to the minute, huh?"

"Always."

James had a brain like a computer and a master's degree

in applied mathematics. Lexie had a little bit of it—she remembered numbers after seeing them only once, which was handy in dispatch—but that's where her math brain ended. Lexie still wasn't sure what James did in his day job, but it was mostly theoretical and had something to do with the planetarium on the hill.

James was very smart. Right then, though, he did not look so. He sat on their mother's red-velvet covered couch, a drink in his hands, his head pitched back, his mouth hanging slightly open. His eyes were unfocused.

"Oh, my gravy, what is that? Scotch?"

He gave a slow nod.

"How many have you had?"

"Just this one. And I've only had a few sips."

"Oh, no." Lexie's heart sunk. "And you look like that already?"

"She's bad today."

"Want to make a run for it?"

"And risk having to hear about *that* for the rest of our natural lives?" James shook his head. "I can't take it. I can't. I'm definitely going to have another one of these, though. I can tell you that much." Pointing to the bottle on the mirrored mahogany bar in the corner of the opulent room, he said, "Want one?"

"Are you kidding me? Yes. No, you stay there. I'll get it."

From the kitchen drifted a high voice. "Lexington, is that you?"

"Why?" Lexie paused in pouring the two fingers of Scotch. "How many times have I told her Lexie? One million times? Trillion?"

"Because it gets to you." James's eyes were closed. "That's why. You were the first born and you bear the city of her birth. Lucky you."

Lexie said, "I'm going to tell her that last eye lift she had made her look like Joan Rivers."

Her brother snorted. "I'll pay you a dollar."

"Make it ten thousand and you're on."

"Lexington! Come in here and help me!"

Lexie had to give it to her mother—even if she didn't want to—her mother knew her way around a kitchen like Lexie knew her keyboard at work. Mira Tindall was known for her four-course meals which she made all from scratch, naturally, during which she never broke so much as a sheen on her forehead. Her mother just had to look at a Beef Wellington for the meat to practically slice itself, perfectly trimmed pieces landing on every plate. If they were in a Disney movie, her mother would be the wicked stepmother who had a magical cooking charm.

"Daddy's favorite tonight," sang Mira in a disarmingly cheery voice. "Orange-roasted duck with a marmalade and soy sauce dressing, and a bok choy salad with a gorgonzola dressing."

Lexie didn't remember this being her father's favorite. In fact, she remembered he'd really liked mac and cheese, the kind from the blue box. He'd make it on nights her mother had taken to bed early with one of her headaches. If Lexie's nose didn't wake her up, her father would gently nudge her after he'd fixed her a plate. Those were her favorite times, growing up. Sitting at the kitchen table with her father—not the fire chief in those moments, he was just her dad—a man who had loved her, no matter what.

Unlike her mother.

"You look pretty tonight," said Lexie.

Mira set down the porcelain gravy boat from which she'd been pouring a glaze over the duck and patted at the bottom of her well coiffed, softly curled hair. It had been red once, like Lexie's, almost as fiery as one of the engines at the station. Now, though, it was a glossy deep auburn, an expensive shade she called "natural."

"Why, thank you. Did you have to add the word 'tonight,' though?"

Naturally, Lexie had already stuck her foot in it. "Sorry. You always look pretty, Mama. You just look even prettier tonight. That color suits you."

It did. Mira also knew style, and the dark plum of her well-cut dress made her petite figure look even smaller. Lexie wondered again what it must be like to have a tummy so flat and small that you never had to suck it in, ever.

Mira wiped her hands on a red cloth napkin that hung from a hook on the huge kitchen island. "Will you get me the dressing on the door of the fridge? The low-fat one."

Ah. The Lexie dressing, careful reserved for her. It was all right—Lexie liked this flavor. She certainly wouldn't complain about not getting the gorgonzola dressing. She knew how this game was played.

Her mother was to be tolerated. Never patronized—oh, no—but accepted. She needed to be listened to. It was simple, if Lexie managed to keep from exploding.

"Good. Carry that in to the dining salon, would you?"

"Can we eat in the kitchen?" Every week, Lexie asked this.

"No," said her mother, just as she did every week.

The "salon" it was then.

"James!" Lexie yelled in her firehouse voice. "*Dinner!*"

Mira gave a long-suffering sigh. "Must you, darling?"

Lexie nodded. "Yep."

CHAPTER 7

Over the main course, Mira quizzed James on his the state of his car. "I saw you, you know."

James made a noncommittal noise.

"Driving on Fourth. You were going too fast."

"Mmmm."

Lexie focused on her duck, which was rich and complex. Her mother had given her a tiny portion, but that was all right—Lexie wouldn't hesitate to help herself to more.

"I want to know when you last washed it."

"A week ago."

"James Tindall. Do not lie to your mother."

"If I tell you the truth, you'll have a cow."

"I don't have *cows*."

Lexie allowed herself a small smile at her mother's distress. Mira did have cows. All over the place, as often as possible. She practically mooed.

James spoke with his mouth full, something designed to make Mira lose it even faster. "I washed it in January."

"But it's *October*."

"So I've heard."

"You can't do that."

"What? Keep up with the calendar? We've been using the Gregorian calendar since the switch from the Julian, in 1592, and even though it's inaccurate, it works for modern civilization, so ..."

"It's embarrassing. I can't have a son driving a car that looks as if you sell drugs from it."

"Whoa, now," said James, who had admitted to Lexie once he'd never even tried pot in his teens. "Did you actually see me selling heroin down by the docks or did someone just tell you I was there? Because that's a lie. I sell over by the bookstore."

Mira's eyes went to slits. "That's not nice. Just wash your car. Your father would have a fit."

"Dad wouldn't have cared," mumbled James.

"He cared about everything," insisted Mira, pushing her plate away with a petulant, delicate shove. "Now I've lost my appetite." She glared at Lexie.

Lexie, ignoring her mother, buttered another piece of bread.

"Darling, I bought that for James."

"You bought a whole loaf of herbed slab from Josie's bakery not intending for me to have even one piece?" Lexie grabbed another slice before her mother could move the plate away.

And in this way, as always, they entered the Lexie portion of the evening.

Lexie could stage it, if it were a play. She could write out the words and block the action. She knew her mother would say things like "a little chubby, don't you think?" and "no boy wants a girl to weigh more than he does." Lexie knew she would respond with curt assents or dissents that

Mira would pretend she hadn't heard. The best part of the night would be when Mira stood, putting her hands flat against her belly. "Do you see this? Do you know how hard I work on this?" Lexie would barely prevent herself from snorting, thinking about the two tummy tucks her already-thin mother had gone through and the fact that food had always sickened Mira, no matter how much she liked to cook.

Mira spent all her time worried about how she looked in the mirror. Lexie had spent years working on herself, on accepting her body as it was. As it looked good. As it wanted to be.

And an hour in her mother's house could put her right back to high-school-level mortification.

Skipping this awful part of Friday night dinner was almost impossible, unless one had a grenade.

She did.

"I'm going on a date."

Mira choked on her sip of wine. "Darling! You're *kidding*. Really?"

"Well played," James said in an admiring voice.

"Oh, Lexie. I can't believe it." Mira pressed a shaky hand to her flat bosom. "Really? And I didn't even set this one up for you! Are you serious?"

It was going to be almost as bad as the weight conversation would have been, but at least it had novelty going for it. "I'm not just making it up, if that's what you're asking."

"Oh, no. Of *course* not. Who is it?"

Crap. Lexie hadn't thought this all the way through. "Just a guy. You don't know him." Lexie didn't know him either. Coin was picking him. He had said he would come in to dispatch the following night and they'd vet each other's online suggestions.

"Not someone you work with, is it? Tell me that's not true."

Lexie bristled. "I'm not stupid. It's not. Completely not. He's in … analysis. Computer. Graphics. Something."

"What a relief." Mira arched an eyebrow at James, as if he would back her up on this one. "I never want you to lose a man the way I lost your father. No men in the line of fire."

Just out of Mira's line of sight, James mimed cutting his wrists with his butter knife.

"Moving on," Mira said. "Tell me about this boy."

"Man."

"Man, then. Who *is* he? What does he look like?"

How did she describe someone as yet imaginary? Lexie reached for another piece of bread, ignoring her mother's wilting gaze. Worse, what if she was deluding herself? She hadn't done online dating in a while—what if she'd run out of Darling Bay men to date? What if there *was* no one else out there, and she ended up paying for Coin to go to Bora Bora with a tiny blonde? "He's medium."

"What does that mean? Is he tall?"

Make something up. Anything. "Not really. Average. Well, pretty tall, I guess."

Mira leaned forward. "More. What color hair?"

"Black. Kind of wavy."

"What else?"

What would it have been like, if her mother had always been this interested in her? Like a girlfriend, like someone she could talk to? "Dark brown. His nose is slightly crooked, but it fits his face. Huge biceps. He's quiet, but he's funny. Kind of hysterical, actually. He makes me laugh, but I think a lot of people don't really get him." A flash of heat raced through her body as she realized she was describing Coin. She hadn't meant to do that.

"How many times have you seen each other?"

A hundred thousand. "None. It's a blind date."

Mira stilled. "How do you know what he's like?"

Lexie's brain scrambled, grabbing ideas and letting them go. She settled for a simple, "It was a very thorough ad."

"An *ad*."

"It's an online date, Mother. Of course it was an ad."

"Does that mean ..." Mira's voice trailed off as if she had to gain strength before going on. "Does that mean *you* placed an ad as well? Like a ..."

"Like a what?" Lexie couldn't even guess where her mother would take it next.

"You know, this fellow in my church group has a son who lives at home. He does something with computers, too. I was going to get his phone number for you. Brett didn't tell me much, but his son sounded lovely even if he is a bit of a loner."

Lexie bit into another piece of bread, barely even tasting it anymore. She stared at her mother without responding.

Mira pointed to the butter knife in Lexie's hand. "Now you're just trying to upset me."

Lexie rolled her eyes. Carefully, she put her knife back onto her plate with a clink, and then she set down the half-eaten piece of bread. "Well, you're easy to upset. I apologize for ruffling your feathers."

"It's just that I want you to be healthy ..."

"I am healthy. I run. My cholesterol is jaw-droppingly great. I told you that." No, no, *no*, she didn't want to go down this road. Not again. She couldn't take it tonight. "And the guy I'm going out with likes a girl of normal weight."

"But ..."

"I'm *normal*, Mother, whether you like that or not. Average is size 12 to 14 now."

Mira gasped.

Lexie met the gasp with a sigh.

James burped and reached for the bottle of wine. "Fill 'er up."

"At least have a salad when you go out with him. Just a salad."

Lexie's head dropped forward. When she lifted it again, she said, "Fine."

Her mother had won. Her mother always won.

CHAPTER 8

"This one." Coin pointed at a woman who looked as if she painted her teeth with Wite-Out.

"No way. What if she bit you?"

"Okay, click that one. I like brunettes."

Lexie peered at the screen. "Is one of her eyes drooping?"

"Are you going to kick them all out of my empty imaginary bed without even letting me read their profiles?"

Lexie took a moment to wonder what that bed might look like. "You make your bed every day, don't you?"

Coin, his elbow on the table next to her laptop, said, "Yeah. Doesn't everyone?"

Lexie made her bed once a week when she changed her sheets, whether she wanted to or not. "Sure. What about her?" She indicated a woman perhaps a little higher on the age spectrum Coin had stipulated.

"She looks good. If I wanted the Early Bird Special and to save money on her movie tickets."

"Don't be mean," Lexie said, but she couldn't keep the laughter out of her voice. Looking at people online had always been interesting, but it had always held a strange intensity, also. It wasn't like meeting someone in the grocery store or at church. You didn't get to interact with them a few times before considering having a private meal together. You had to look, read, and then project your entire life—marriage, babies, death—based on what his favorite band was. She could tell Coin was quickly learning that. He'd found a woman he liked the look of, and he'd been excited when she liked Beck. "I like Beck!" he'd said. Then he'd gone on to read that the woman worshipped Beck, and went to every single one of his concerts, and her number one goal in life was to get her hands on a backstage pass, and then to get her hands on Beck's personal backstage. Coin had tilted his mouth to the side. "That's not good, is it?"

"No," Lexie had said gently. "Click the next one."

An hour later, Coin had the hang of it. He'd even reached the point of explaining it to her. Lexie leaned back in her seat to enjoy it.

"Look," he said. "I get it. You go to their profile, and you decide if there could be something there, based on surface impressions."

"Based purely on shallowness, yes. Why don't you mansplain it to me some more?" She was teasing him. Of course looks were the first thing a person noticed. She found herself looking at the back of Coin's neck, where his tee shirt lay along his shoulder. A cord of muscle ran out of his short sleeve. His hands were sure on the computer now, pointing and clicking.

"Hey, have you been working out?" she asked.

It was an honest question—it looked like he had—but he laughed her off. "Okay, I get it. I'm shallow. But you have to have chemistry, right?" *Click, click, click.* "There are a few cute girls on here, but I have to say, a lot of them are just kind of ..." He paused, and clicked a few more. "Not."

Lexie inhaled sharply. Her own profile was on the screen in front of him. They hadn't talked about it yet—she hadn't shown it to him.

He clicked past the picture of Lexie and to the next one, a pretty brunette with a short bob and red lipstick. "I guess this one's not bad."

Lexie waited for him to laugh. Then she would punch him in the shoulder for being stupid, and they'd get on with their browsing.

"Nah," he said. "She's a vegan. Good for her, but I need my bacon on Saturday mornings." He clicked past three more.

He didn't say a word about flying past her own picture.

While he was talking about the *Nots*.

Lexie's stomach hurt, twisting into an acidic knot. The back of her throat tightened. He wasn't joking. He wasn't playing a prank on her. He'd looked at Lexie's picture, and he hadn't recognized her. He'd thrown her right to the bottom of the pile with the other girls who weren't pretty enough.

911 rang.

Lexie lunged for the button, grateful for the ringer's blare. So grateful she didn't have to speak to Coin. Because if she'd had to, her voice would have wobbled, she knew it.

As it was, her clear, strong voice said, "911, what's the address of the emergency? Okay, tell me exactly what happened."

CHAPTER 9

Lexie had gone weird there, at the end. Right when 911 had rung. Usually if firefighters were in dispatch and they ended up being the ones assigned to the call, she'd shoo them on their way even before she dispatched them to it, smiling as the waved them out the door.

But she'd gone all mechanical. Answering the call—a man choking on a meatball—and dispatching Coin's engine without meeting his eyes. Sure, she was also giving the wife medical instructions at the same time she was banging out the engine and the rescue, but Lexie could usually do both those things while waving and taking a sip of coffee. Maybe she knew them or something. They were just around the corner from Lexie's house, after all. Maybe they were favorite neighbors. That must have been it.

By the time Engine One got on scene, Lexie had talked the wife through the Heimlich, and the meatball had been expelled. Even though he was fine, Rescue One still transported the patient to the hospital, because he asked to go. In a British accent, the old man had pointed to his throat and said, "It's still in there. 'Ospickle. I want to go to the 'ospickle to make sure she did me right. Maybe she kil't me."

The wife had folded her arms across her broad chest and said, "I saved your bloody life, man. I did you more right than I done in years. You should thank the men, you ingrate."

Coin's favorite part of the job was the interaction with patients. This wasn't true of all his coworkers. It used to be that men—and back then, it was all men—wanted to be firemen because they wanted to fight fires. The fire service had attracted a certain kind of man with a specified skill set.

Times had changed. Instead of taking care of loved ones at home, people today relied on the fire service for medical care. People called 911 for things like migraines and turned ankles because they didn't really know what else to do. And over the same few decades, buildings had become safer. Every new house and business in Darling Bay had to have sprinklers installed. Its attic might burn, but the house itself would be saved. True, they did have their fair share of older buildings with poor wiring, and there would always be the idiots who used cheap extension cords, but nowadays the fire service was primarily a medical organization. More than eighty percent of their calls were medicals now, and the older firefighters who hated that fact were reaching retirement age. The new, young guys, the eager-beaver twenty-one-year olds, were coming in with their paramedic licenses in hand, knowing how to start IV lines better and faster than the guys who had thirty years on the line.

Medicals were what Coin loved, the face to face, the way he could make people's days better. No one called the fire department because they were having a good time. Everyone needed help at some point. Most people—and this still surprised him—apologized for calling, for interrupting the firefighters' routine. "I'm so sorry you had to come out. You have better things to do." They didn't realize that *this* was what they did. What they'd signed up for.

"It's no problem, ma'am." He gave a small nod of his head to the patient's wife. For a quick second he felt like doffing his invisible cap at her, and then realized it must be because of her British accent.

Back in the engine, Tox said, "Pizza? I don't want to eat Luke's chicken. Did you see how much red pepper he put on that?"

Coin took the right turn instead of the left that would bring them down to the wharf and Junior's Pizzeria. "I gotta get back to the station."

"Why?" Hank asked from the back. As usual, his headset crackled. He was the most junior so he had to use the worst headset in the rig.

"I got a couple of things to do." Coin had to figure out what had been wrong with Lexie when he left. Had he screwed something up? She was the one who wanted him to go online, right? This whole dating thing had been all her idea, after all. Had he insulted one of her friends or something?

When it came to Lexie, he didn't want to screw up one single thing. She was too ... something. Coin didn't want to name what it was. Come to think of it, he couldn't.

Tox sighed heavily into the mike. "You have to get back to dispatch."

Coin hit the brakes at the light too hard.

Tox said, "Geez, man, chill. What's wrong with you? What was Lexie saying to you back there?"

"Why?" Coin watched the light carefully, as if it might turn a new color any minute. Purple. Pink.

"You usually come out of dispatch with a smile. And now Lexie is all stink-pants on the radio."

As if from a mile away Lexie could hear them, her voice came over the radio. "Engine One, status check?" It was her annoyed voice. She didn't use it often, and because of that, the guys took it seriously.

"Did you hit the available button?" Coin pointed at the computer on the dash.

Tox said, "Crap."

Hank's voice crackled over the headset, "Ever since you and Grace got together, dude. You're off your game."

Tox twisted in his seat. "You want to say that to my face?"

Coin knew Tox was all bluster. And Hank was right. Ever since Tox fell for Grace, he'd been softened. A couple of his rough edges had been smoothed off. Coin approved. "You gonna answer dispatch or not?"

Tox clicked the radio button. "Engine One clear." He released the button and spoke into his rig headset, so only Coin and Hank could hear him. "She knows that. She can see where we are on the computer. What I don't get is when dispatch asks us stupid questions that they already know the answer to, like they're trying to trip us up. Especially Lexie. She's not usually a witch like that."

Coin took the turn onto Lowry Avenue.

Lexie's voice filled the cab. "Engine One, check for open mike."

Coin felt a sick chill. "Tox," he hissed.

"It's not me." Tox held his hands up. "I'm not touching anything."

Hank said, "Dude. You're sitting on it. Your shoulder mike fell off."

Tox undid his belt and scrambled in his seat. Replacing his shoulder mike, he said, "Well. That sucks."

Hank said, "You *so* owe her a coffee."

Coin groaned. It had been Tox's voice, but their engine. She knew they were talking about her. It was going to make whatever was going on in her head even worse.

They owed her more than coffee.

He turned on his left signal.

"Where are we going now?"

"Apple pie. And strawberry ice cream."

"Yeah, man," said Tox, his voice chastened. "I'll buy."

"Yep. You will," agreed Coin.

Lexie was still in Coin's profile. What she *should* do was insert something into the profile she'd written for him. Instead of "occasional life saver," she should put "occasional jerkwad." Instead of five foot nine, she should put that he was five one. For fun, she typed, "My feet stink but since I leave my shoes on for sex, you'll never know."

With a grim smile, she hit save.

For one second, Coin was available for dating on the internet with really stinky feet. It felt pretty good.

But it wasn't fair. She erased the sentence and hit save again. He was back to being almost perfect. If it wasn't for him having a kid, he would be pretty completely irresistible. Some women were going to dismiss him because he was a father.

But others? They would love him for it. They'd see his Brady Bunch potential. A ready-made family.

Gah.

And he'd flipped right past her picture.

She went to her own profile again, seeing it as he would, from his profile.

Lexie had thought it was a good picture. Her brother had taken it in his backyard as she helped him prune the roses that had gotten completely out of control. She'd had her hair piled messily on top of her head, yeah, but that was par for the course. One long curled strand was falling over her eye, and she was laughing, her mouth open.

When she'd posted the picture, she thought her eyes looked like the eyes of someone having a good time. Someone fun. Someone who could be attractive to the opposite sex. She'd gotten some "likes" from a few men just in the couple of days it had been up.

Coin had flipped past it. Right past it. Hadn't even slowed down. For Pete's sake, she'd been wearing a short-sleeved striped T-shirt, and her tattoo could be seen winding down toward her wrist.

How could Coin have not recognized her?

Was it possible it *was* a joke? Maybe he'd been planning on exclaiming, "Just kidding! Cute pic, Lex," before she answered 911. For one second, Lexie let herself hope.

Then she gave it up.

He hadn't been going to do that.

It hurt. Anyone else could have flipped past her picture and she wouldn't have cared. For some reason, though, the fact that it had been Coin stung. Deeply.

The door to dispatch slowly opened.

Tox poked his head around the corner even slower.

"Permission to enter?"

Lexie sighed. "Why do you want to come in? To talk to a witch? You sure you didn't mean there to be a letter *B* at the beginning of that word?"

Tox held the door open for Coin and Hank who slunk in behind him. Coin held a pie in his hands. Hank was juggling a quart of ice cream back and forth.

"We brought you pie and ice cream."

"Good." Lexie wouldn't forgive them this easily. It had hurt her feelings, what Tox had said. She tried to be the best dispatcher in the department. She tried to be professional on the radio at all times. And still they talked crap about her.

"Dude, we're sorry," said Hank.

"Dude," echoed Lexie. "Whatever. People always ask, but *this* is why I never date firefighters." It wasn't, but it sounded good.

Tox put the plates he'd brought on the counter, and Coin started slicing pie.

"What if I told you I didn't want any?" asked Lexie, crossing her arms.

Tox laughed.

Coin said, his voice kind, "Of course you do. You love apple pie, especially Josie's."

Lexie softened, as if her insides were made of the same pink ice cream Hank was scooping onto each plate. That pie was special—Josie put something into the filling, something with a kick, almost as if she put a dash of cayenne in with the cinnamon. Whenever she was asked, though, Josie said it was just something she'd never had a recipe for. No one believed her.

Lexie reached forward and took a forkful. She couldn't help it—she moaned. "It's warm. Did you nuke it down the hall?"

Coin shook his head. "She'd just taken it out of the oven."

"You are forgiven." She took another bite. "In fact, you could swear at me on the radio. You could tell me I have no idea what I'm doing—" she glared at Tox "—which is pretty much what you did, and I'll forgive you every single time. As long as you bring me this."

Tox ran his finger along the edge of the plate, where the syrup had dripped down. "We are sorry, though. We were just venting."

Lexie pointed at the steam coming out the top of the slits in the pie crust where it hadn't been cut yet. "That's venting. What you were doing was being a jerk. But I don't care." She took her plate with pie and ice cream to her terminal. "Now get out of here. I want to enjoy this in peace, and I have to go to bed soon. Megan's getting up in thirty minutes."

Coin frowned, meeting her eyes for a moment.

No. She didn't want to deal with him.

"You, too. Go."

Coin said to Hank and Tox, "I'll meet you down there."

"Coin ..."

"We have to finish the thing."

Tox and Hank didn't even bother to pretend to act interested. "See ya. Sorry again, Lex."

"Fine, fine," she said as she pushed another forkful of heaven into her mouth. It really was fine. How many times had she cussed the firefighters out for being stupid? It was only by the grace of a kind heaven that she hadn't accidentally stepped on the foot pedal when she'd been saying it.

When they were gone, Coin sat next to her again, as if he hadn't left, as if he hadn't gone on that last call.

"You know what the worst part is?" Lexie asked.

Coin looked at her, his eyes soft, as if he were really listening to her. She normally loved it when he looked like that. This was her friend. A man she trusted.

"The worst part is that I saved that guy's life. The wife had no idea what to do."

"And we didn't even say that." Coin looked stricken. "We just forgot. Tox was so upset by what he said on the radio—"

"In his conversation to you two," Lexie clarified.

"That we forgot to confirm you had a field save."

Lexie shrugged. "Well."

"Good job," said Coin, his voice warm. "He didn't seem like the most healthy kind of guy. I think he'd already had at least six or seven beers by the time he choked on the meatball. If you hadn't talked his wife through the Heimlich, it would have probably gone a lot worse for him, later."

Lexie looked at her lap. It had hurt her feelings, yeah, hearing them talking crap about her. But it hadn't hurt as much as it had that Coin had passed right by her photo, not seeing her as pretty or special in the slightest.

Lexie sighed. "I'm tired, Coin."

"Can we just finish this?" He reached forward and touched her upper arm. "I'm not good at this personal ad stuff, and it's making me nervous. I like looking at it with you."

But instead of drawing his hand away, his left it on her arm for a moment. His hand was wide, and warm. Solid. Lexie wanted to lean against it. His touch sent a jolt straight down her spine, and she got warm from the inside out. Steam. He created a column of steam in her. When did *that* start?

"Fine. Let's get this over with." Lexie moved so that his arm fell from hers. "I responded to a girl I thought you might like."

"You responded as me?"

"That okay?"

"Yeah." He sounded delighted and scooted closer. "Show me who you chose."

Why on earth was this making her so nervous? "This one. Ginger."

"Is she a redhead? I love redheads."

Lexie pushed at a red curl that had dropped over her eye. No, he didn't. He liked pretty girls, and not for their hair color. "Strangely enough, she's not. She's a brunette."

From the ad, Lexie had decided that Ginger was the total package. Her ad was smart and even self-deprecating. She seemed funny. She was a home-health aid, so she would understand shift work. "Look, she's in the medical field."

But Coin's eyes hadn't gotten to the reading part. "She's *hot*."

"I know," said Lexie. "You don't think I know what you like?"

Ginger looked like the girl in the Vampire Diaries, thin with long, perfectly straight dark hair. She had eyes that were dark pools of emotion, and high cheekbones. In the picture, it didn't look as if she were wearing any makeup, but her lips were shiny, her skin completely flawless. It was a demure picture, no bending forward for this one, no décolletage on display. But just from the swell at the top of her pretty black blouse, it was evident that she had the goods, too.

She was perfect for Coin.

"What did you say in my message to her?"

It hadn't been a long email. Lexie didn't think Coin wanted to get into a major online flirtation. The point was to meet someone fast, wasn't that right? "You said that she had struck you with her beauty but what was important to you was that she takes care of other people. And that you'd like to take her to dinner some night."

"Holy crap. I'm good." Coin grinned, but he looked nervous at the same time.

Lexie smiled back at him, feeling tired to her very soul. She would have stood up to refill her water, but she was too exhausted.

Coin grabbed her bottle and filled it, as if he'd heard her thinking it. He was good that way—he always had been. He was going to make some lucky girl a really great boyfriend, Lexie knew that.

"Now you," he said.

"Nah," said Lexie. "I'm tired. Let's do it tomorrow."

"You helped me. Now let me help you."

"Coin, I'm really too tired. I don't want to look at one more picture, and I don't want to read one more little white lie. I don't have the discernment left right now to figure out that if a guy says he's outgoing it just means he's trying to cheat on his wife."

Coin said, "Then it's my turn. Log in to your profile, and let me keep your laptop while you're sleeping."

Lexie stared at him. "Are you crazy? I'm not giving you my laptop."

"Too much porn on it?"

"No!"

"Then log in to your profile. I trusted you to send an email on my behalf, and it sounds like you did a great job. Why won't you let me do the same for you?"

"Because."

"You don't think I'm a good writer? I'm good." He paused. "I'm good enough. Log on."

She just looked at him.

He gestured. "Lex. You're my best friend. Trust me."

Lexie did trust him, that was the thing. He was a good man.

She logged on. Her profile populated the screen.

"There you are!" Coin smiled and pulled the computer toward him.

Then he paused.

A moment passed. And another. Coin stared at the picture of Lexie smiling, that old rose behind her, the rose that matched her tattoo.

"That's you."

"Yeah," she said.

Coin did that drawing-in thing he did sometimes, as if he were pulling an invisible blanket around his shoulders. Usually Lexie hated seeing him do it. This time, maybe, it was okay.

"Oh, Lexie."

Megan entered dispatch, her dark hair sticking straight up.

"It's fine, Coin. Find me a love match, okay?" She didn't look behind her as she left the room.

CHAPTER 11

He was a monumental jerk. A idiot of mountainous proportions.

Coin had flipped past her picture while he'd been dismissing women as not right for him.

The irony of it.

And the actual truth was that he'd seen the photo and while he hadn't really looked at it—not close enough to recognize her—he'd been drawn to it. Almost enough to stop and look some more. But he'd kind of thought it reminded him of Lexie, and that would just be weird, scamming on a girl while Lexie sat next to him. So he'd kept clicking instead of noticing—like any other person with a correctly-working brain would have—that it *was* her.

A snore sounded, so loud it practically rattled his bed frame. Eight people was a lot of people to sleep in one room, even if that room was separated by head-height walls. Most of the guys were all right, but Mazanti snored his head off when his allergies were bad. Guaranteed, tomorrow Tox would make him take his allergy medication before bed.

It was fine, anyway. Coin wasn't sleeping anytime soon.

He had a mission, and he'd accomplish it tonight. He owed her that. Heck, the truth was that Lexie deserved happiness, plain and simple. And if he could help her find that, he'd be happy.

Why, then, did he want to growl every time he found a guy who looked like he might be perfect for her? Coin kept clicking. Punishing himself for being such a weasel earlier.

Man, *look* at that guy. Coin supposed a woman would find him good looking, if she liked big white teeth and a smile that looked like he'd just won a ski competition. Almost every photo of the man was in the snow. Lexie wouldn't like that. She hated being cold. At work, she was usually cuddled up to her space heater. Once she'd even caught her department-issued blue sweater on fire when she'd hung it off the back of her chair and placed the heater too close. She'd blamed it on the department for buying shoddy uniforms, and the dispatchers had been upgraded to wool sweaters after that, something that he remembered had pleased her no end.

He'd always suspected her of catching it on fire just to get rid of the acrylic. Coin smiled, and clicked away from the stupid ski bum.

Flip, click, flip. No, no, no. No to the orange man who looked like he fake-baked most of his waking hours. No to the mechanic—nothing wrong with the profession, but the man couldn't tell the difference between their and they're, and Lexie would rip his grammar to shreds in a heartbeat. Lexie needed someone genuinely intelligent.

Coin wished for the millionth time that he'd finished college. He'd come so close, but then his family had fallen apart. In his senior year at college, his mother had called him, her voice shaking. She'd asked him to come home, even though it was a three-hour drive

When he'd gotten home after forcing his rattling Plymouth to go as fast as he could make the beater move, he'd found his mother bruised almost beyond recognition. Her cheek was concave, sunken, from where his father had hit her so hard. She'd need three rounds of surgery just to put her face back together.

It had been the first time he'd ever hit his father back. It had felt too good, smashing his fist into his father's mouth—feeling the pain bloom, flaring up through his knuckles. He'd heard his father's teeth break. It was about time. By that point, his mother had two bridges in her mouth from the years of abuse. Coin himself had a metal rod in his right arm from the time his father slammed him against the car door and then shoved it closed on him.

During his whole childhood, Coin had hidden from his father, staying quiet, making himself as small as possible. It was the only thing that had ever worked for his mother, and he imitated her until that day his rage was too great, until the day he hit him.

Then he knew if he saw his father again, if he had to look at his mother crying even one more time, he'd end up killing the man. Happily. Gratefully. He could do it with his bare hands. He knew he could, and the knowledge terrified him. Not even the threat of prison scared Coin. Maybe in jail he could hit more people like that with some level of impunity.

He decided to be a cop. He did a couple of ride-alongs with the local police force before seeing the truth—that too many cops became police officers for the exact same reason he was considering it. So that they could exact justice on the street, before any judge or jury could show up.

After he witnessed a police officer he'd considered to be a nice guy deliver a "bonus" hit to the ribs during an arrest, he'd applied to the fire academy. At least if he became a fire-fighter or a paramedic, he could not only bandage the victims but maybe counsel them on how to get out.

Even though he loved his job, he still regretted the lack of a college diploma. Having that would have made him feel smarter and maybe, if he had the extra brains, he'd know how to do this. How to find the girl of his dreams the perfect guy.

He clicked on the next candidate.

A podiatrist. The dude didn't look like he looked at feet all day—he looked like a guy who could grill a perfect burger while holding a beer in one hand and kid-wrangling with the other. His ad was spelled correctly. More than that, it was funny and modest at the same time. He poked fun at himself.

Lexie loved people who could laugh at themselves.

Coin sighed. Mazanti's snore rocketed through the dorm and someone else yelled a garbled threat for him to knock it off. The air conditioner kicked on with a whine. Coin stared at the beige curtain that divided his bed from the hallway and flexed his fingers. Then he typed. "Hi. My name's Lexie, and I'd love to get to know you a little more."

For punishment, it sure was working.

CHAPTER 12

S erena answered Lexie's knock.

"*Finally*," the girl said. "You're here. Dad's in his bathroom freaking out about a tie or something. He's, like, sweating. You have to help him."

Good. Maybe Coin was as nervous as Lexie was. She'd been in a mild state of panic all afternoon leading up to the double date. It didn't make sense. Lexie was normally good at this stuff. She usually didn't think about dates until an hour before, and then she went through her closet and pulled out the cleanest dress that both still fit and that she hadn't worn in a while. Even if she looked at herself with her mother's eyes every time she passed a mirror—wide hips, big breasts, too much tummy—she was usually able to silence Mira's voice in her head, making herself feel comfortable in her skin again. She was on the pretty side of tolerable, yes. And she knew how to dress. It was simple, really. Lexie actually remembered the day she'd finally figured out her style. She'd pulled on a dress that showed off her rack, and then she'd pulled on a pair of cowboy boots. It took her approximately seven seconds to dress, and she felt great.

But today? Why was it that she could handle a regular date just fine, but pair it with another couple? Lexie was a wreck. She'd gone through her closet and tried on every single dress she had. All of them were wanting in one way or another—the red one was too short, and she'd probably show off her underwear if she sat down. The black polka dot dress was too long and made her look twenty years older. The yellow low-cut dress was TOO low cut and might get her arrested for indecent exposure. The green and black dress was too high necked, making her look like someone who would hush children in an arcade.

She'd tried jeans and T-shirts, but rather than coming across as fun-loving, as she'd wanted to, she'd come across as slovenly. Each T-shirt she owned had something wrong with it: a tiny rip at the belly (how did she *do* that?) or too floppy at the neckline. She didn't even own that many good T-shirts since she had so many department issued ones.

With seconds to spare to get out of her house and to Coin's on time, she'd thrown on her favorite outfit. A simple wrap dress—black and red—with her everyday black cowboy boots. She hadn't wanted to wear it because Coin had seen her in this getup a zillion times. It was her go-to, what she threw on when she didn't want to think.

But then again, the date wasn't with Coin, was it?

It was, however, at his house. "You're asking too much of me," he'd said, "To not only go on a double date, but to do it in public. You love my backyard."

It was true, she did. With a sprawling lawn, a covered patio with surround-sound speakers, and a hot tub that sat ten, she'd spent many a night drinking beers with the other members of A shift behind Coin's house.

He'd continued, "And I love my backyard. We don't know these people. We need the home team advantage."

"Because we're going to play touch football with them?" she'd asked.

He'd brightened. "Yeah! I could take a podiatrist."

Lexie had told him in no uncertain terms that there would be no touch football on a double first date.

Now, Serena turned her head, and said, "Come *on*. He won't mind."

Coin wouldn't mind if Lexie barged in on him getting ready? She wasn't sure about that.

"I'll wait in the kitchen." She raised the bags. "I have things to put away and get ready, anyway. Want to help?"

Serena nodded and yelled, "Dad! Lexie's here! Hurry *up*!"

In the kitchen, Lexie got out the ingredients for her mini caprese salad. "Look, I'm going to skewer all this stuff with toothpicks."

Serena's eyes lit up. "I wanna stick things, too."

Lexie showed Serena how to spear a cherry tomato, then a ball of mozzarella, then a piece of basil. They piled them on a plate. "Later," Lexie said, "I'll drizzle them with olive oil and salt."

Lifting one eyebrow just like her father did, "And you're calling this a salad?"

"Maybe more like an hors d'oeuvre."

"A *what?*" Serena looked at her like she'd said a bad word.

"It just means an appetizer."

Serena thought about this and then seemed to decide it wasn't important enough to pursue. "So you're not on the date with my dad tonight, is that right?"

Lexie poked her finger with the toothpick. "Ow. No. Not really."

"What does *that* mean?"

"It means we're sharing a date. I'll be on a date with a guy, and he'll be on a date with someone else, and we'll all hang out together."

"Me and my friends hang out all day at school. Why isn't that dating?"

Lexie knew Serena understood what a date was. "What's eating you, kiddo?"

Serena frowned. "I just don't want ..." She trailed off and sighed heavily.

"You don't want him to date? Is this about your mom?"

"No." Serena looked at Lexie as if she were stupid, which Lexie had to admit, she felt at that moment. "It's not about my *mom*. It's about my dad. He's isn't ready."

Oh, that was cute. Lexie smiled. "You want to take care of him."

Another long sigh. "It's not that. I just don't want ..."

Lexie took a guess. "You don't want him to get hurt."

Serena stared at the cherry tomato she'd just poked multiple times. "When Mom and him broke up, he was sad for like fifty years."

"Well. Maybe not that long, considering you're eleven, but—"

"You know what I mean. He's not that tough."

The words were surprising, coming from Serena. Didn't all little girls think their fathers were gods? Tough as nails?

"I mean," continued Serena, "He saves lives all the time. Remember the time he pulled that guy who weighed, like, a ton, out of that fire?"

Lexie did remember that. Hearing Coin's voice on the

radio as he labored to breathe in his SCBA, as he announced he and Tox were trying to make their way out of the house, was one of the scariest moment she'd ever had on the radio, and she'd had plenty in her time. "Yeah. He's good at his job."

Serene nodded somberly. "He sees people actually die, did you know that?"

"Yeah," said Lexie. She wanted to touch the girl, to reach out and put her hand on her shoulder, but they didn't have that kind of relationship. They were buddies. Not huggers. "I know. It's something I'm glad I never have to do."

"Because you're on the phone."

"Yep." Lexie heard people die. That wasn't uncommon. But she never had to see it.

"So I know that makes him strong. He's stronger than most men, I think," said Serena.

Lexie felt a warm glow in her stomach. That was Coin, all right. "What's worrying you, then?"

"What if he falls in love?"

That was the whole point of their plan. Lexie would never tell her that, of course. "What if he does?"

"No one is going to be good enough for him."

"Oh, I'm sure there's someone out there." Really, Lexie wasn't at all convinced of that herself. "What are you doing tonight?"

"Mom'll be here soon. She's taking me to the movies and then tomorrow we're making waffles, even though she's not eating gluten right now." Serena gave an eleven-year-old eye roll.

"How about this? I promise I'll vet whoever your dad dates." She'd been planning on doing that, anyway.

"Vet? Like a veterinarian?"

"Different word. It means I'll test them. Make sure they're good enough for him."

Serena's dark eyes met Lexie's. In them, she could see Coin's intensity, and something that was the little girl's own strength. "Yeah. I guess you'll do okay at that."

"Thanks." It felt strangely reassuring to hear.

"You let me know what you find."

Lexie saluted smarted. "Wilco."

The doorbell rang, and Serena grabbed her backpack and ran for it, yelling goodbye at Coin as she went.

The front door slammed.

Lexie poked another tomato with a toothpick.

Coin entered, his hands at his throat wrangling his tie. "Where'd she go?"

"She left."

"She didn't even kiss me goodbye," Coin said sadly.

Lexie needed a knife and reached around Coin to get one out of the drawer. She felt as comfortable in this kitchen as she did in her own. Impulsively, she pressed a kiss against Coin's cheek. She meant it lightly. A joke. The kiss he didn't get from his daughter.

But the way it felt—Lexie didn't see it coming.

Coin's skin was smooth, as if he'd just shaved. He smelled of shaving cream and something spicy.

He froze when her lips touched his cheek, like she'd turned him to stone. In turn, Lexie stilled, too. Everything went silent except for the blood rushing in Lexie's ears.

Coin turned his face and met her eyes. They were less than two inches apart. If he leaned forward, or if she did, their lips would touch.

In a low voice, Coin said, "You shouldn't have done that."

Lexie felt herself heat, deep, low inside. A shiver danced through her, a quicksilver quake of excitement.

Then nerves took over. She stepped backward, knocking the knife against the counter on accident. "You're right. I'll end up cutting off my hand or something." *Lighten the moment.* She needed to bring it back to what it always was, two friends, comfortable with each other. Hanging out. Waiting for their respective dates to arrive.

Coin didn't move with her into that lightness. His eyes held hers, and she could almost feel the heat radiating from his body. "Lexie—" he started.

She fumbled with the plastic bag on the counter. "So I marinated the thai beef all afternoon and it should be ready for you to throw on the grill when they get here. Did you remember to buy the bean sprouts?"

Coin leaned forward, placing both hands on the counter. Lexie watched his knuckles whiten as he grasped it. A muscle jumped in his jaw.

Then he exhaled, and it was okay again. "Yeah. In the fridge. What should I do about this friggin' tie?"

Lexie smiled, trying her best to make it a normal one. "Take it off. You don't need it." He didn't. He looked amazing as he was, in the light blue button-down shirt with thin gray pinstripes. He wore dark gray pants with the creases still in them. "You look great."

His smoky gaze met hers again. If he did that much more, she'd have to rethink this whole double date thing. How could she flirt with someone else when her friend—her best friend—was pinning her down with that oddly hot stare?

She held up the knife and pointed the tip at him. "Cut it out, dude."

"What?" Coin blinked, as if waking up.

"You're being weird and I don't like it."

"I'm not doing anything."

"You're looking at me funny."

"Like how?"

She drew a circle in the air with the knife. Honesty was always best. "Like my dress is too low. It's kind of freaking me out." She glanced down. "Oh, dang, *is* it too low?"

Coin cleared his throat and didn't say anything.

She tugged at the vee of the dress. "Get me a safety pin."

"No."

"Excuse me?"

"Your dress is fine."

"You've seen it a million times," Lexie said. "Why are you staring at me like that?"

Coin seemed to shake himself. "Sorry. Maybe I'm nervous."

"No. Get over that. Right now." She tapped the cutting board with the knife. "And please give me the mint from that bag. I have things to chop." He didn't get to be nervous. She wouldn't let him. "It's going to be a great night. I *will* it to be a great night."

CHAPTER 13

It was a terrible night.

Ginger arrived first. She was as beautiful as her picture had been, like someone from a magazine plopped down in his house. She adored her job, in which she took care of a woman with late-stage cancer, and spoke in glowing terms of her family. Her laugh sounded like bells.

Coin loathed her. He preferred people he understood. People who had things wrong with them, who were self-conscious and made mistakes. Perfect people couldn't be trusted.

Within minutes of stepping through the door, Ginger was in the kitchen, dancing around Lexie like they'd been friends for years, mixing a drink that combined sweet vermouth with mint and bourbon. How did women do that? How did they become best friends within seconds, smiling and laughing with each other as if they were on a date with each other?

Well, shoot. He supposed they kind of were. After all, Lexie had chosen her, right? It was Lexie who'd done the corresponding, who'd sent that first email.

Thomas arrived next. He was tall and looked like some Clark Kent wannabe, all the way down to the chunky, hipster glasses. Sure, Coin's clothes were good, too, as nice as this guy's, but he knew he didn't look comfortable in them. Coin felt best when he was in a firehouse T-shirt and cargo pants, clothes that had been washed a million times and gave comfortably when he moved. The shirt he wore tonight was so crisp he could hear it whooshing as he moved his arm to shake Thomas's hand.

"Come on in. I'm Coin. Should we call you Tom?"

"Thomas, actually," he said smoothly. "I've never liked Tom."

Neither did Coin.

In the kitchen, the women greeted him with a handshake, but in the case of both of them, Thomas followed up the handshake with a kiss on the cheek. It was smooth. Both women smiled.

Great. Now Lexie had kissed both of them on the cheek tonight. And she was only on a date with one of them.

"Get you a beer, Thomas?" Coin gestured with his own bottle.

"Actually, Lexie mentioned that we'd be eating Thai, so I brought a bottle of white, a nice vintage I picked up the last time I was driving through Napa. My friend owns the winery, and this is a special reserve. They only bottled a hundred of these, and I think the ladies might enjoy it." Thomas gave Lexie a toothy smile. "May I open it and pour you a glass?"

"Sure," said Lexie, her voice a little breathy.

Coin reached for the wine opener. "Let me. This opener can be a little tricky."

"Oh, no problem." Thomas took it from him smoothly.

"I'm good at this." And he was. A flick and a twist, and the bottle stood open.

Nosey, the cat he'd rescued from the tree years before, wandered in, yelling for food. This might be good, Coin thought, as he watched Thomas eye the cat. Nosey wasn't particularly friendly, and he didn't like strangers.

But then Thomas said, "Gorgeous beast. Can I give him a piece of cheese?"

"No," said Coin.

"Of course!" said Lexie, handing him a small ball of mozzarella. "Coin, don't be mean to your cat."

"Watch out," Coin said reluctantly. "He bites." Hopefully, that was.

Nosey—traitor that he was—took the cheese from Thomas and then wrapped himself around the man's ankles. So much for loyalty.

Lexie took a sip of the wine Thomas had poured for her and sighed. "This is wonderful."

"I'm so glad," said Thomas. "So, will you show me the garden, Lexie?"

The garden? Coin bristled again. It was *his* backyard, not hers. "I'll go with you. I need to check the grill."

"I can do that, if you like. Happy to help," said Thomas.

Of course he would. He'd probably be happy to save Lexie from a speeding bullet, too.

"I got it," Coin growled.

While Thomas ambled with Lexie through the back part of the yard—down where the jasmine was, Lexie's favorite flower—Coin scrubbed the grill. Black ash flew from the grate and landed on his shirt. Brushing it off, he just made it worse, grinding the ash into the weave of the fabric.

"Great," he muttered, taking a long, deliberate pull on his beer. What kind of jerk brought white wine to dinner? And knew the vintner?

It was his fault. He'd picked the guy.

He heard Lexie laugh at something Thomas said, and it was her real laugh. The big one, the one she let out when she was surprised and delighted by something. It never failed to make him feel like a million bucks when he got her to laugh like that. Thomas sure seemed to have brought it out in her quickly.

Fine. The grill was clean. Thomas and Lexie were hitting it off.

He'd go hit it off with Ginger, then.

By the time Thomas and Lexie came back into the kitchen, Coin was putting the food on the table and counting the minutes until the night was over. Ginger was delightful. Everything she said was sweet and kind and generous. Just to test his theory, he asked if she did any charity work in her free time.

"Oh, yes," she said with an enthusiastic smile. "On Wednesdays and Fridays, I work at the soup kitchen in Eureka. Just in my free time, you know."

Yep. She was fantastic. And absolutely, thumpingly boring. Coin nodded, attempting to look interested.

They sat at Coin's dining table. For one brief second, he felt embarrassment that his napkins looked as handmade as they were. Serena had made them—yellow and polygonal—when she'd been briefly obsessed with sewing. When Thomas shook one out onto his lap, he raised one eyebrow.

The embarrassment faded and pure pride took its place. That's right, his daughter had made the funny-looking napkins. Because she was *awesome*.

As if Ginger could hear his thoughts, she said, "What about you, Coin? You have a daughter, right?"

"I do." What if he faked a migraine? Lexie wouldn't buy it—he'd never complained of one before—but would she blow his cover? She might. She seemed to be enjoying Thomas's company quite a bit, if you could judge that by the number of times she reached out to touch his arm as she laughed.

"Tell us about her." She sounded genuinely interested.

Coin gave Ginger a second look. A real one. It was rare enough to find a woman willing to date a man with a kid, and even rarer still that she sounded interested. And with that long dark hair, and those snapping, sparkling eyes—this woman could get just about any guy on a string.

Why, then, was it that Coin couldn't keep his eyes off Lexie? For one night, you'd think he could fake it, but no. He couldn't.

Lexie filled in the awkward pause that had happened while Coin had been thinking. "Her name is Serena. She's eleven, technically, but could pass for thirty in terms of world awareness. She says she wants to be an artist or a baseball player, but I think she's going to be a writer. Every single second she has to spare, she has her nose in a book." Lexie smiled warmly at Coin. "She's supremely great. And Coin is amazing with her. They're the best pals, except that he takes care of her, too."

Coin got it.

He was on the wrong date.

Ginger and Thomas should be gazing into each other's eyes, preferably at a restaurant far, far away. And he needed to be on a date with this woman. Lexie. Yeah, he could admit he'd always had a crush on her. Every firefighter at the station knew that and teased him for it, though he always denied it. It was time to admit it.

He wanted to be alone with Lexie. Really alone. Man and woman alone. In his mind's eye, he pictured Lexie leaning close to kiss him smilingly ... He needed to nuke this stupid date. There had to be a way.

He would *find* a way.

CHAPTER 14

Something was wrong with Coin, and Lexie had no idea how to fix it. It must have had to do with what she'd said about Serena because that's when he'd gone all weird, but Lexie couldn't figure it out. Should she not have bragged on his daughter? Shouldn't that have been a *good* thing to do in front of his date?

Instead, he'd gone all quiet. Spooky quiet. Lexie had seen him silent many times, but not like this. He put off a dark energy, a kind of pulsing, low-grade anger. Ginger, appropriately, seemed more interested now. Of course. Women always loved a brooder, right? Earlier, when Coin had been chipper, Ginger had been merely sweet and polite. Now she gazed at him between sips of her wine, as if she wanted to be the one to make him talk.

Well, screw that. Lexie was his actual friend. It was her job to find out what was wrong with Coin. In the meantime, though, he had to pull himself together.

She kicked his ankle, hard.

"Hey!" said Coin.

"What?" asked Lexie innocently. She gave him a look. *Talk now or I will kill you later.*

Coin seemed to get it. He started flirting with Ginger. Lexie was amazed by the change in him. Even when Thomas asked her direct questions, she kept half her attention on what Coin was saying. She should have been happy. Instead, she just felt more irritated. She gulped wine to try to cool her temper and ended up spilling it down her front.

If someone had been watching their table, they would have seen a perfect-looking foursome, though. Coin got almost gregarious, and Ginger got even prettier under his attention. And Thomas, it turned out, wasn't the bore that he looked—he'd spent time in Guatemala and had hair-raising stories that kept them all entertained.

All Lexie wanted was for them to leave.

She stood and started clearing plates. Ginger, who was still picking at her salad—of course she was, the waif—looked surprised when Lexie swooped it away, but she didn't protest.

"There's dessert," said Lexie brightly. "You all just stay right here, and I'll get it ready." She wanted to be away from all of them. Maybe in the kitchen she could grab the deep breaths she so suddenly needed. Sitting next to Coin as he flirted with Ginger had done something to her, something she didn't like.

"Please, let me help," said Ginger. In any other circumstance, Lexie would have claimed this funny, interesting, pretty woman as a new friend. Now? She wanted to jab her with a salad fork.

"No, thanks. You just sit there and look pretty," Lexie said. As if stick-thin Ginger could do anything else. She probably woke up pretty. *Her* eyes probably never got puffy with tiredness or dark with allergies.

In the kitchen, Lexie ran the water good and hot to rinse the plates. She wanted her hands to sting. She wanted to feel something other than this ridiculous, petty jealousy.

Behind her, the kitchen door swung open. Coin set two more plates on the counter.

"I got it," said Lexie shortly. "You just go out there and flirt." She couldn't help adding, "You're doing a great job at it."

Coin turned and leaned with his back against the counter. He was inches from her, and it was making her nervous.

"Am I?" His voice was low.

Holy Helen, he looked good in that button-up shirt. It pulled against the width of his broad shoulders. The fancy clothes made him look like someone else. Someone who would have a great time on a date with someone named Ginger.

"Ow," she said. The water was so hot it made her eyes water.

Coin reached in front of her and turned it off. "Stop," he said.

"I'm almost done."

"Me, too," said Coin.

Lexie's eyes widened as he put one hand behind her neck, turning her away from the sink to face him. Her back was against the sink, and he caught her there, trapped between his body and the counter.

For one desperately long moment, Lexie wondered if she'd misunderstood something. Maybe this was how Coin always told women not to do his dishes. Maybe there was something she was supposed to say so that he would burst into laughter and she would be able to breathe again.

Instead, his eyes got darker. "I'm sorry," he said. "But there's no way I'm not kissing you, darlin'."

Then he did.

Lexie—if she'd ever taken the time to wonder what it would be like to kiss Coin, which she hadn't—would have thought it would be nice. Sweet. A charming kiss, perhaps. She would have thought Coin would be a kind, considerate kisser, echoing the way he was in other parts of his life.

She would have been dead wrong.

Coin kissed her hard. Fast. It was a kiss that was made to melt the kneecaps of the one kissed, and sure enough, Lexie found she had to reach her arms around him to keep herself standing. His mouth was hot, *so* hot against hers, and when she parted her lips at his insistence, she felt his tongue meet hers. He knew exactly what he was doing. He tasted of beer and need, and then all rational thought left her head.

All she knew was that the way he moved his mouth on hers was making her certifiably crazy. She wanted more, more of his lips, more of his tongue. He nipped her bottom lip and she gasped so loudly she wondered if Thomas or Ginger could hear her losing her mind.

She pulled her mouth away and stared at him. "We're on *dates*."

"We sure as hell are."

"With other people!"

"Seems that way." He traced her wet lip with the pad of his thumb.

"We can't do this."

In answer, he lowered his mouth to hers again. More insistent this time, he kissed her harder, as if he was challenging her. Goading her.

That wasn't fair. Coin knew better than anyone else how much she liked a challenge.

So she kissed him back, for all she was worth. She swept the tip of her tongue along his upper lip, a lick and a promise, and then plunged her hands, still wet from the dishes, into his hair. She couldn't help the low moan she let out, a sound he matched. He pressed himself against her harder, and while the counter dug into her back, Lexie didn't care, because she felt him against her, hard and needy, just like his mouth. She grabbed the front of his shirt and pulled, knowing in the back of her mind that her lips would be swollen from this kiss, that there would be no way to hide it.

And still she didn't care. Why hadn't she ever kissed him before? Why had she wasted her time with *not* kissing him?

Coin pulled back with a curse. "We're being rude," he said.

Lexie made a noise that was half gasp, half laugh. "You think?"

"I'll handle this," he said.

Lexie rubbed her lips with the back of her hand, grateful she'd only worn lip gloss, now long gone, and not a telltale lipstick. Then she followed him into the dining room.

"Sorry, folks," said Coin, but he didn't sound sorry at all. "We just both got paged to work."

Ginger's eyes narrowed, and Lexie could practically see her doing the math. "Really? I didn't hear any beeping."

Coin shrugged. "Phones are on silent."

Thomas recovered more quickly, and while he was putting on his light jacket, he said, "Lexie, this was too short. Can I call you tomorrow? Maybe take you to that new Burmese place on Route 119?"

Lexie opened her mouth to answer but Coin beat her to it. "No," he said.

"Excuse me?" Thomas looked surprised. Ginger may have already figured it out, but Thomas was slower on the uptake.

"No, you can't call her."

"And why not?" Thomas widened his stance, but though he was tall, Coin still had an inch on him. Lexie couldn't help feeling a little embarrassed for him. She should step in. Coin was being unbelievably rude.

And it was completely *fascinating*. Lexie didn't want to move a muscle or say a word, she just wanted to watch. And breathe. Maybe she could get her heart rate to slow down a little.

"Because you're not her type."

Thomas laughed, but it sounded thready. "And what's her type?"

"I am," Coin said. "Go away."

CHAPTER 15

Coin closed the door on Thomas and Ginger. Maybe in front of the house, as they discussed their host's rudeness, they'd exchange phone numbers and hook up. He did feel sorry for them, but hey. They'd gotten dinner and a show.

He turned the deadbolt, slowly. Somehow, he needed to put off the next moment, when he would turn and meet Lexie's eyes. What if she was furious? He'd seen her mad plenty of times, but he didn't want her to be angry with him over this.

Not this.

When he turned, though, she was closer than he'd thought she was.

And she was just standing there. With that look. One hand twisting a corkscrew curl the way she did when she was flustered, she just looked at him.

He didn't know whether to apologize for being a huge jerk or to kiss her again. And the longer he took to decide what to do, the closer she probably got to leaving, so he said, "Do I need to say I'm sorry?"

Lexie tilted her head.

"Because I will. If that's what you need." He sat on the couch with a thump and kicked his feet up onto the coffee table. Yeah, she'd kissed him back in the kitchen, but he hadn't given her much choice. What kind of kiss was that? If she wanted to yell at him, he deserved it.

"Why did you do that?" She pulled that curl again, and it was possibly the cutest thing he'd ever seen a woman do.

"I don't know." That was a lie. He knew why he'd done it. He'd kissed her because the thought of her kissing Thomas was too much to bear. Because he should have done it years ago. Because way too often, when he closed his eyes at night, her face was the last thing he thought of.

Because he would never, ever be able to admit that to her.

"Was it because you were trying to show off?"

"What?"

"In front of them. You were all put off by Thomas and his job, and you had to prove you didn't like him, so you kissed me."

If Thomas had talked about his podiatry business, Coin hadn't heard it. Of course, pretty much any time the guy had said anything Coin had tuned out, so he'd missed a lot of the conversation. "That wasn't it."

Lexie sighed impatiently. "Then what was it? Why did you *do* that?"

"Why do you sound so upset about it?"

"Because I am," she said. "That wasn't fair."

"Who said life was fair?" It was a line he'd always hated when his dad had said it. Coin had managed successfully to never say it to his daughter, and here he was, trotting it back out for Lexie. He wished he could take it back, but it was too late.

Lexie blew out an exasperated breath. "I don't understand you tonight."

"Tonight?"

"Stop it."

"Stop what?" Man, he was being a jerk. And he couldn't quite seem to cut it out.

"This." She waved her hands at him. "This whatever you're doing. This isn't my Coin."

Her Coin? That was rich. "You don't know the first thing about me."

"I know you better than anyone else."

He leaned his head back and closed his eyes. "That doesn't mean much." He felt her sit on the couch next to him, and it was all he could do to keep his hands on his lap, to not reach for her.

"Then tell me," she said softly. "Tell me what's going on with you. I don't get it."

"You."

"What?"

Coin kept his eyes closed. "You're going on with me."

"Me?"

"Lexie Tindall, I've liked you since we started working together."

"Me, too. You're my best friend."

Great. In a second, she'd probably pat him on the head. "I don't want to be your pal."

"What *do* you want?"

He opened his eyes and leveled his gaze at her. He wouldn't give her half truths now. "I want you. I've always wanted you, Lexie." He watched her lips part in surprise, and he continued. "I want you in the morning, and I want you before I go to sleep. On my days off, I save up my best stories to tell you. When we're at work, I have to stop myself from sitting in dispatch all day, just to watch you work. When you work overtime, I leave my radio on so I can listen to your voice." He curled his fingers into fists to keep from touching her. She was just a breath away, a breath he shouldn't take. "I can't stop thinking about you when I'm not around you, and you make me completely freaking insane when you pull on your hair like that."

Her hand dropped to her side, and the curl bounced back into place. "Why are you telling me this?"

"Because I'm freaking sick of lying." He tried not to think about how bad it would be at work when she hated him for this.

"Are you drunk?"

"No!"

She let a pause hang between them. "Coin, I don't know what to say."

"Admit that you were kissing me back in the kitchen."

She blinked. "I was. I did."

Happiness burned a trail through him.

"But," she went on, "I didn't know what I was doing."

"You seemed pretty comfortable."

"It's *you*. You're my *friend*. I don't kiss my friends. Or my coworkers. Or any firefighter, *ever*. You know that."

Coin wanted the look of confusion on her face to clear. He'd gone too far to turn back now. "Tell me you don't feel something between us." He could feel it at that exact moment, a heat, an incredible tension that almost shimmered visibly in the air.

"You're imagining it," she said slowly, not meeting his eyes. "There's nothing between us."

No. She had to feel it, too. "Come on, Lexie. Don't pretend like that kiss in the kitchen wasn't life changing."

Lexie pushed a hand through her curls and then touched her bottom lip. "It was just a kiss, Coin."

If she was saying that, if she *believed* that, then Coin had just been proven to be a huge fool. Everything he thought existed between them, didn't. He'd imagined the whole thing. "Oh."

"I should go," she said, standing.

He moved to join her.

"No, don't. Where's my purse? Here it is." She grabbed it off the floor. "I brought that pan, but you can bring it to me at work later."

Her words were fast, tumbling over each other. Her voice, usually clear and calm, was high pitched and tense. "Lexie, don't go. Let's talk about this."

"Nothing to talk about, Coin. You have a little crush. You'll get over it, and then someday we'll laugh about all this."

Coin touched her arm and said, "Don't leave."

Her face tilted up to meet his eyes. Six inches, that was all that separated them. He waited for her to come to him. Taking the kiss from her hadn't been fair. He wouldn't kiss her again until she kissed him first.

Her eyes were sad. Had he done that to her?

"It was just a kiss," she repeated. "I have to go."

CHAPTER 16

There were few things good about a knock at the door at 7 a.m. on a day off, but the worst part of it was that Lexie knew who it would be.

She was right.

Her mother stood on the doorstep, a basket in hand. "May I come in?"

Lexie stood the door open and turned around, going into the kitchen. She poured water in the carafe and didn't ask her mother what she was doing there. She'd know soon enough.

"You haven't even made coffee yet?" Mira sounded incredulous.

Lexie did a half turn to show her mother that she was still wearing pajamas. "I hadn't gotten up yet, either." She'd been lying in bed, thinking about the kiss from the night before. About Coin.

Mira pointedly looked at the watch on her slim wrist. "You know what they say about the early bird."

"I don't like worms," said Lexie. "They're slimy."

"Your date. Tell me."

Oh, crap. She'd forgotten she'd told Mira about her blind date. "It was great." And by great, Lexie meant horrible. Thomas had been a bore, she'd been horrified at how amazing Ginger was, and then, out of nowhere, Coin had kissed her.

He'd kissed the blazes out of her. And worse, she'd liked it.

She'd loved it, actually, although she hadn't told him that—she couldn't. That was only the second worst part of it, though.

The very worst part was that somehow he had feelings for her. Feelings! For Lexie!

Lexie knew Janice, Coin's ex-wife. She'd been a perfect firefighter's wife—pretty and popular. She was a tiny little thing. Petite. She had birdlike wrists that looked as if she wouldn't be able to wear more than one bracelet at a time.

For that reason, Coin had always existed in Lexie's mind as someone who liked a thin woman. She'd never thought, even idly, what it would be like to kiss him, although apparently she should have.

All that he'd said? About feeling that way for her for so long? It couldn't be true. It just wasn't possible. When Lexie was at work, she felt like she was camping. Being at work for two days straight didn't lend to marathon makeup sessions. She didn't do her hair. The guys had seen her a million times in the middle of the night, bleary eyed with lack of sleep, and she'd seen them the same way. There was no romance at the station.

That was how she thought about work. That was how she thought about *Coin*. As a friend.

Such a good friend.

Why, then, could she still feel him on her lips? Why was it she could still taste him, feel the weight of his mouth on hers?

And why had she had so many dreams about him all night? In the most disturbing one, he'd pulled off her dress and touched her in the places she'd never imagined Coin touching. She'd wanted him to. Then he'd disappeared, and she'd heard his voice, calling out for her on the radio. She'd known he was trapped, pinned, hurt somewhere, and she couldn't help him. She'd woken with her hands shaking and tears on her cheeks.

Lexie put the coffee into the filter and hit the red button. Behind her, Mira twittered about something, flitting in and out of the kitchen. She'd settle soon enough, and Lexie would have to listen. But now, as she leaned against the counter—which reminded her of how she'd leaned against his sink last night—she put her fingers to her lips.

Online, men who liked big women just came right out and said it. In fact, men online were often disappointed that Lexie didn't weigh more, which was always a strange kind of treat. Online dating meant she could weed out the ones who had issues with bigger girls. "Please be height/weight proportionate." If Lexie knew one thing, she knew that's something she was. Her round curves suited her frame, they always had. It had taken years and years for *her* to accept them, especially with a mother like Mira always chipping away at her, but finally, she was okay with what she had to work with. Her weight was truly appropriate to her height and frame. She was strong and fit.

But height/weight proportionate—to men—meant thin enough to disappear while standing sideways.

Coin had put that in his ad.

What if he'd stopped kissing Lexie because he'd felt her love handles? What if he hadn't followed her outside when she left last night because he was mortified by his mistake?

How on earth was she supposed to go back to work tomorrow?

Mira flitted back into the room, rubbing oil into her cuticles. "You know, I just love that manicure set I gave you. Don't you?" Mira reached out and grabbed Lexie's hand, looking carefully at the chipped nails, at her old, worn-off polish. "Honey. That just sits in your bathroom, and you don't even use it. Let's go get mani-pedis today! Together!"

"No, thank you."

"Why not?"

"No, thank you." Sometimes that was all she could say to her mother, all she could think of saying. If she kept repeating it, kept saying no without explaining why, she knew from past experience that eventually her mother would give up and start bugging her about something else.

Mira poured herself a cup of coffee and sat at the table.

"Will you make me a slice of toast, darling?"

"Yes," said Lexie. That she could do.

"Gluten-free?"

Lexie didn't bother answering. The regular kind of bread—full of delicious gluten—would be just fine for her mother.

"Now tell me about the date, darling, from start to finish. No, just one piece is fine for me."

It wouldn't cross her mother's mind that perhaps the other piece of bread might be for Lexie. She pressed the toaster's button, folded her arms, and turned to face the music that was Mira Tindall.

"I didn't tell you, but it was a double date."

"Oh! How interesting! Why?"

"Safety in numbers."

"What is this fellow's name again?"

"Thomas."

"A good, strong name."

It wasn't. It was a little boring, Lexie thought, especially when contrasted to a name like Coin. "We had dinner. That's all."

"You said it was great. What made it that?" Mira leaned forward, her eyes alight. "Did he kiss you?"

Lexie paused. Thomas hadn't.

"He did! He did. Was it a good kiss?"

The best kiss of her life, maybe. That's why it was so upsetting. "Ma, I'm sorry, but I'm not that into telling you about *any* kind of kiss."

Mira frowned. "Now you're just hurting my feelings on purpose. I just want you to find your *always*."

Crap. She'd meant to head her mother off at the pass, not to hurt her. "I'm sorry. It just feels weird."

But sheesh. Her "always." It had been her father's favorite word. He said it to Lexie when he kissed her good-night and told her he loved her. "Always," he'd whisper with one last kiss pressed to her forehead. It was the last word he always said to her mother before he left the house. "Always," he'd say before smiling at her and shutting the door.

Yeah, sometimes Lexie dreamed about an "always." But she also dreamed about pregnant giraffes chasing her in off-road vehicles. She didn't put that much stock in dreams.

Still looking pained, her nose tilted higher than normal, Mira reached for the basket she'd brought. "I'll give you your present and then I'll leave, and then you can get back to your day that I'm so obviously interrupting." She sent a pointed look around Lexie's kitchen. "Or you can go back to sleep. It's all the same to me, obviously."

Inwardly, Lexie sighed. "Thank you."

"I haven't even given it to you yet."

With this kind of lead-up, Lexie knew she'd hate the present. "I'm sure I'll love it."

Mira clapped. "Oh, you *will*." She took out a package and unwrapped the red cloth around it. "It's herbal. The woman who sold it to me swears by it, and you should have seen her cute little figure. She said it will cut the craving for all fats and sugar by ninety percent if you just drink a cup of this every morning and then again before you go to bed."

"It's a diet supplement?"

"Aid, darling. It's a health aid. Everyone needs a little help now and again." Mira tilted her head and examined Lexie. "You look like you've put on just a *skosh* more weight again. I thought you told me you'd keep that five pounds off. For your health."

Lexie sucked a sip of coffee into her mouth even though it was still too hot. "It's not for my health," she muttered, knowing better and doing it anyway.

"Excuse me?"

"You hate that I'm not tiny, like you."

"Don't be ridiculous." But Mira's smile was too bright.

Lexie stood up. "I will never be anything like you. And you know what? I don't want to be." She willed herself to stop talking, but she couldn't seem to find the off switch. "You're too small."

Her mother preened like a peacock. "Thank you."

"It's not a compliment."

"Your father liked me trim. Sometimes, I think that if you ..."

"Lost weight I could catch a firefighter? Like you did?"

"No!" Her mother looked genuinely horrified.

"Dad loved me, too. Just like this."

"But—"

Lexie said, "I'm the way I am *because* of you. Because of the fact that you've never been healthy a day in your life. If you have a piece of candy, you have to punish yourself for three days. You know what that does to a kid? Whenever I had a piece of birthday cake at a kid's party, you'd make me run around the block ten times before bed for a week."

"For your *health*."

Lexie pushed forward, gripping her coffee cup handle as if it could save her. "Healthy is eating sensibly. You were anorexic and bulimic when you were in college." Her mother had admitted it only once, when Lexie had caught her vomiting in the bathroom at a dinner party.

"But I haven't been since then. I'm just very careful to watch what I eat."

"Last Wednesday? Eating an apple for your one meal of the day isn't careful."

Mira sniffed, but the whites of her eyes looked panicked. "I shouldn't have told you that. I just didn't have much food in the house last week and I didn't want to go shopping."

"You bragged about it in order to make me feel bad."

"I didn't." Mira rewrapped the tea in the cloth.

"I'll never be you." She said it as gently as she could. "Do you know how hard I've worked on being okay with myself? Finally accepting myself? It's taken years. And therapy. And lots of friends loving me for exactly what I am."

"I know—but now that you're dating more ..."

"Lots of men love a girl with curves." Lexie's voice had a

wobble now, and she wished with all her heart that her mother would just leave.

"Sure." Mira's head bobbed again. "Sure."

Her mother left quickly, saying something unconvincing about a charity meeting. As the front door closed, Lexie could almost hear her father's voice. "Always."

It sounded like a reproach.

CHAPTER 17

Station One was directly on the route between Serena's school and her mother's house, so she often stopped by to see Coin on his work days.

Today Coin had plans for his daughter. Coin realized he was scheming to use Serena to get the attention of a woman, romantically. That probably made him some kind of unfit father. But then again, Serena was going to end up with a bag full of oatmeal raisin cookies, her favorite, so he supposed that made up for it. At least, he hoped it did.

Serena was suspicious, though. "You want to bake cookies here at work?" From the day room, the baseball game blared. Hank and Tox yelled at whatever play their guy had just screwed up.

"Why not?"

"What if you get a call?"

"Then you can stay in the station and make sure the cookies don't burn."

Serena poked the room temperature butter with her finger. "I thought when you guys got a call that the oven shuts off."

"It does." It was a fire safety thing—if they had to go on a medical or fire run while a pan of eggs was on the stove or a loaf of garlic bread was in the oven, the fire station wouldn't burn down in their absence.

"So that won't work."

"But if you stay behind, you can turn the oven back on. If you can't fix a problem, you're not trying hard enough."

She narrowed her eyes. "I hate it when you say that. I don't know about this."

Coin was flummoxed. "You don't know about baking cookies? That's what you're telling me."

Holding up a finger she said in a voice that was strangely grown up, "One, you don't normally bake cookies at work. Two, you're *weird* today."

"How weird?" He crossed his eyes and stuck out his tongue, but Serena didn't laugh.

"Oh, I get it," she said, throwing her backpack onto the kitchen island.

"What?"

"That date you had two nights ago. You're making *her* cookies."

"Why can't I make my daughter a treat if I want to?"

"Because you don't," she said simply. "Mom makes cookies. You and I go out to ice cream. That how this works."

It was true. That was the division of labor that had come to pass over the years.

"So you're getting your daughter to make cookies for the girl you like."

Coin rubbed his face. "Yes."

She laughed, a child again. "That's so cute! Let's bake!"

The engine—of course—did get a call between the baking of the second and third trays. It was just a woman who cut herself shaving but was on blood thinners, so the clean up took longer than Coin would have liked.

When he finally got back into the station kitchen, the oven was off. Two trays of cooling cookies sat on the big wooden island. Coin knew that with the guys coming back from the hospital, they'd last about five minutes, so he piled a plateful and headed to dispatch.

Laughter filtered down the hall. Good. Lexie was awake, then. Nerves raced down his spine. He'd pointedly stayed out of dispatch today until now. That in itself was enough to look suspicious, but he hadn't wanted to arrive empty handed.

"Dad! Lexie's playing poker with me!" Serena was standing next to Lexie's computer, bouncing on the balls of her red sneakers. "Look! Look! I won fifty bucks!"

Coin leaned in to look and caught a breath of Lexie's scent, light and floral. "Tell me that's not real money."

Lexie said, "I know we get away with a lot here, but I'm pretty sure the chief would frown on gambling while on the job."

"Lexie said she always wins when she plays poker with you," Serena crowed, picking up a still-warm cookie from the plate.

"Only because she cheats," said Coin. He held the plate out to Lexie.

"She said it's because you have no poker face. But I don't really know what that means."

Lexie took a cookie. "It means he can't hide anything." She paused, as if weighing the cookie in her hand. "I just realized I might be wrong about that, though."

"Okay, Dad, I'm going home." She grinned at him. "And tell me how taking those cookies to the girl goes. Be nice. Make her laugh."

"Wilco," said Coin, kissing her on the top of her head as she raced past.

"Bye, Lex!"

Lexie waved and then leaned back in her chair with a sigh. "That girl has energy."

"Enough to power the sun," agreed Coin. "Hi, you."

"Hi." Her eyes dropped to the cookie plate. "Serena said you were baking cookies for Ginger. She had the clever thought after you left that you should have baked gingersnaps. But I bet Ginger might have heard that one already, huh?" Her words fell faster than normal, as if she was nervous.

"She got it wrong."

Lexie bit her cookie.

"I said I was baking them for the woman I liked."

Lexie started coughing.

"You okay?"

She nodded, holding up a hand. Good grief, even red faced and sputtering out small pieces of oatmeal raisin cookie, she was still sexy. A trio of long red curls fell in front of her eyes as she coughed, and she didn't push them out of the way. She hid behind them.

Coin's heart beat faster. This was when she told him to stop, to leave her alone.

But instead, she only said, "She didn't tell me that part."

Incredibly heartened that she wasn't—yet—tossing him out on his ear, Coin said, "I guess she left that for me to do."

Lexie gestured to the plate he still held. "You can put that down, if you want."

"Yeah." Coin felt about thirteen years old and just as smooth.

"You made my favorite cookies."

"You always say they're your favorite but you only like them when they're fresh. Homemade."

She laughed, and her eyes danced this time. "I swore to Megan before she went to bed that I could smell cookies baking, but she told me it was just wishful thinking."

Coin shook his head. "Nope."

"Thank you."

She had no idea how welcome she was.

Maybe it was time to tell her again.

"Lexie," he started.

"Look," she said. "About what happened—"

"Can I say this first? And then you can tell me what you think? I'd let you talk but I'm so nervous I feel like I might pass out, and if you had to call the guys down here to evaluate me, I'd have to quit and then I'd have no way to pay the bills and I'd end up living in my car, which would be fine most of the year but it's coming up on winter and—"

"Coin. Say it."

"When I kissed you, that was exactly what I'd wanted for a long time. A really long time. I'd imagined kissing you a thousand times, and when I did, it was better than anything I'd ever been able to conjure with my mind. However ..." He picked up a cookie, broke it in half, and then put it down again. "I know that's not for the workplace, though."

"Coin, it's ..."

"I promise to be my regular self while I'm at work with you. Just me. We do the crossword puzzle in the morning and I bring you coffee in the afternoon."

She touched the newspaper. "You didn't come in this morning."

"I know."

"I couldn't get 11-down."

"Me, neither."

Her gaze rose to meet his. "You did the puzzle without me?"

Pointing, he said, "So did you."

"Oh."

Slowly, Lexie said, "You said you're yourself when you're at work. What about when you're not at work?"

Coin turned a chair backward so he could straddle it. He looked right at her. "All bets are off. I pursue you."

CHAPTER 18

The way he said it—Lexie had never heard Coin speak in that particular tone of voice. As if he knew exactly what he wanted and how to get it, and as if what he wanted was her.

It was so *hot*. Good grief, she was still thinking of Coin as hot. She'd been hoping she would get over it. Apparently she hadn't. "So you ..."

"I call you. I ask you out on dates. If you say yes, then we go."

Would he kiss her again? At the end of a date? Lexie made the mistake of meeting his eyes, and she found the answer there. He would. He would kiss her senseless, until she lost her breath and her reason and everything else she felt as if she'd left behind her at his house.

"What about the bet?"

He shook his head. "What?"

"The Bora Bora bet. On who falls in love first."

"Oh, yeah," Coin said.

"And?"

"I'm hoping I get to take you to the islands."

He wasn't touching her—still five feet away—and she gasped as if he had.

Coin went on, "But that doesn't mean you should stop trying to find your perfect match."

She frowned. Now she was confused. "Wait ..."

"I know this isn't your idea. I'm just telling you I'm not scared of who you might meet online."

"So you want me to date other men, too?"

He shrugged. "Sure. Go on as many dates as you want. Hey, if you meet the love of your life and he's someone else, I'll pay for your vacation."

"All that dating just sounds like a lot of driving." She meant it to be light, a joke, but he took it seriously.

"No driving when we go out. I'll drive."

Amused, Lexie said, "So you're one of those? A guy who thinks he needs to be all macho and open my doors and everything?"

Coin leaned back in the chair and kicked his work boots out in front of him. A lock of dark black hair brushed his forehead. He needed a haircut and, since it was late afternoon, a shave. He looked hot as sin and twice as dangerous. "Yeah."

Lexie took a moment to imagine what it would be like if she crawled into his lap, wrapped her arms around his neck, put her mouth on his ...

Then she wondered if the chair was rated for two full-grown people. It would be just her luck that the chair would break and she'd land on top of him, breaking him. Then again, Coin was strong. She'd seen him in the halls after working out. Those muscles he carted around were no joke, his calves sculpted, his biceps defined.

"Okay," she managed. "I don't need you to open my door. But I suppose I would let you do it if you had to."

He grinned, and she noticed that he had a dimple in his chin. Why hadn't she ever noticed that? "I'll call you tomorrow. When we're off. And I'm going to ask you out."

"What—"

"And you can tell me your answer tomorrow. Whatever it is. When we're at work, we're just at work. Normal."

———

LEXIE WASN'T PLANNING to tell a soul. Not one person.

But Megan was so ridiculously receptive to other people's emotions that she walked in, put the backup pager in its charger, took one look at Lexie, and even though Megan's eyes were still bleary from sleep, demanded, "What happened?"

"Nothing," said Lexie, diligently pulling up her work email, hoping something critical had been sent to her inbox, something that she'd have to work on immediately.

"Don't lie. You're a bad liar."

"I'm a *good* one."

"Nope, you suck. Did you have a bad call?"

"No."

"CPR?"

"No."

"Something happened."

Lexie rested her head on the table top next to the keyboard. "Coin has a crush on me."

Megan flapped her hand. "Oh. I thought something had *happened.*"

"You knew?"

"Who didn't?"

"Um, me."

"Do you return the sexy feelings?" Megan reached up in the cupboard for her tea but as usual, she was too short to reach.

Lexie took down the box of tea for her. "Why do you keep it up there?"

"I put it on the low shelf every week, and every week Sue puts it on the top one."

"Why don't you just ask her to quit putting it up high like that?"

Megan arched an expressive eyebrow. "And start world war three? You know what she's like. Anyway. You didn't answer my question. How do you feel about Coin?"

911 trilled. Lexie lunged for it, catching it on the first ring. It was only a quick question about fire extinguishers, though, and the caller was directed to call fire prevention. "Nine years of doing this and I still can't believe people call 911 for that kind of thing."

"I can't believe the police dispatcher transferred it! Now. About Coin."

"You're a dog with a bone."

"For good gossip like this?" Megan sat at her terminal, lowered the rack of monitors in front of her, and stared happily at Lexie. "You can call me any kind of dog you want."

"You tell anyone, you die."

"Honey, like I said, everyone knows—"

"No one knows that he kissed me at his house Wednesday night."

Megan made a locking-her-lips-throwing-away-the-key move. Then she leaned forward. "More."

"That's it."

"*More.*"

Lexie couldn't stop the smile that spread across her face. "I liked it."

"Of course you did. He's hot."

"You think so?"

"Coin Keefe? Who doesn't think so? And?"

"I can't stop thinking about him now." She covered her eyes with her hands and then peeked at Megan. "About my coworker. I always said I'd never date a fireman. Not after Dad ... Anyway, they're too ..."

"Life-savey?"

"Yeah."

"Too handsome in their turnouts?"

Lexie smiled.

"Too kind to old people and children?"

"Yeah, yeah," Lexie laughed. "I take your point. But what about you, then? You never date them, either."

"Honey, I hate firefighters." But Megan's smile took the sting out of the words. "Cockier bunch of men you'll never meet. More, please."

Lexie felt herself blush. "He said he's going to ask me out."

"You going to go?"

Slowly, Lexie nodded.

"Oh, girl. You're in so much trouble."

Lexie put her head back down on the counter. "I know," she mumbled. And inside her, deep inside her bones, she felt a burst of something that felt like joy mixed with fear. It felt like elation.

CHAPTER 19

As good as his word, Coin called the next day. Lexie thought about letting his call roll to voice mail. *Chicken,* she thought. She answered.

"Do you want to go out with me tonight?"

"Yes."

A silence. Then Coin said, "Wow."

"What was I supposed to say?" Lexie gripped the phone.

"I just didn't expect you to agree so easily."

"You gave me enough warning." She'd laid in bed for hours last night, thinking about him. About this moment.

Coin laughed, his voice low. The timbre of it sent an unexpected shiver through her. He said, "I won't next time."

The shiver went deeper.

"Seven. I'll pick you up."

"What should I wear?"

"You'll look great no matter what." His voice was so confident she almost believed him.

Just Coin. It was just Coin. A date with him would be

like doing the crossword. Or playing poker. Friend stuff. It would be normal.

Or like juggling fireballs.

At six p.m., Lexie started getting ready, telling herself it was ridiculous to start so early. At 6:45, she was sweating and cursing herself for not starting earlier. She'd tried on every outfit she owned, including outfits which were either twenty pounds too tight or twenty pounds too loose.

She finally went with a lemon boat-necked shirt that made her hair look wildly red in contrast and her favorite pair of jeans. Once a guy at the gas station had remarked on the way they fit her, and she had to admit, while looking over her shoulder in the mirror, they suited her backside.

Then there was the makeup question. Normally she only wore lip gloss and that was only on days she felt fancy. Coin was used to seeing her bare faced. But makeup made her feel more confident. She put on eyeliner. That looked good, a bit more sophisticated. She added mascara. Okay, even better. Maybe a little eye shadow, lemons and plums. Then she added blush, and a lip stain that promised to be kiss proof.

Looking in the mirror, she had the sudden fear that she looked like her own slutty twin sister. That hadn't been her goal, but her doorbell was ringing and she had no time to wipe any of it off. She wasn't even sure if she *could* wipe off the lipstick. She might have permanently berry-stained lips now.

Coin stood on her porch like it was a regular thing, when in fact Lexie realized he'd never been over. She'd been to his house many times—poker games and movie nights with the rest of A shift—but Lexie couldn't remember him being at hers.

"Hi," she said.

"Howdy," Coin drawled.

Lexie's heart thumped. "You've never been here before, have you? Come on in." She was proud of the way she'd decorated her little bungalow with cheerful colors and easy-to-live-in furniture. Her father had dabbled in painting, and while he'd never been very good, she loved his work. It was bright and loud, just like he'd been. The paintings looked good on her walls. It felt like home. The house might be a little untidy, but it was clean, and it was all hers, something she was proud of.

"Sure," he said, following her inside. "But I've been here before."

"You have?"

"You had the flu. Two or three years ago. I brought you the turkey pot pie from Mabel's Cafe."

"Oh," Lexie said. So he'd not only been to her house and she didn't remember, but he'd come over when she'd been looking her absolute worst, all red-nosed and snotty. "That's right. Anyway," she gestured around the living room. "This is the place."

"Mmm." Coin nodded, not looking anywhere but at her.

"What?"

"You look pretty."

"I don't look like a hooker?"

Coin's look of heated intensity crumbled and he whooped. "No. Why?"

"Because of all the makeup. I think maybe if I walk downtown, I could pick up a client or two."

"You'd have to wear higher heels than that," he said. "And I'd recommend a short skirt instead of those jeans. But yeah, you'd get some business."

Suddenly conscious of the fact that they were

discussing her getting paid for sex, Lexie blushed from the roots of her hair to her toes. No, this wasn't fair. She wasn't supposed to be the one who blushed—*Coin* was. He was the shy, quiet one. Not her.

Grabbing her wallet, she said, "I'm ready."

"Good," Coin said. "Me, too."

Lexie knew that sound in Coin's voice. He had it on the radio when he got on scene first at a fire and took incident command. He got that sound when he was telling his daughter on the phone that it was her bedtime and that she should stop arguing with her mother.

He had it now, too. He was determined and ready.

Lexie felt as if she were holding invisible sparklers as they stepped off her deck into the evening.

CHAPTER 20

Coin had cleaned out his truck, throwing out the litter Serena left behind her, but it was still awkward as they drove.

"Nice night." It was probably the dumbest thing he'd ever said in his life.

"Mmmm."

He didn't know how to talk to her. Not like this. Not on a date. At work, yeah. He could—and did—spend hours in dispatch talking about nothing in particular and everything in general. Didn't matter if it was a political argument or a limerick contest, the thing he liked best about Lexie was that she always seemed to want to listen to him.

She *really* listened. And she didn't let him get away with anything, either. When his voice dropped because something was hard to talk about, she called him out on it.

"You're good to talk to." His voice was too loud in the cab of truck and Lexie jumped. He didn't blame her. The comment came from silence, out of nowhere.

"Um. Thanks?"

Perfect. Compliment the woman on how good she was

to talk to when they *weren't talking*. Now *this* was the dumbest thing he'd ever said in his life. Who knew he could top himself twice in two sentences?

One night, about five years ago, he'd been sent on a vehicle versus pedestrian call. The engine beat the rescue squad there, and Coin was the first person out of the rig. The little girl who'd been hit while riding her bike had been about the same age that Serena had been then, maybe six or so. He'd looked down at the child, lifeless in his hands, and for one long minute, maybe sixty seconds or so, her face changed in front of him. When he looked down at the girl, he couldn't see her—he could only see Serena's face. It wasn't something he was imagining. She didn't mildly resemble his daughter. For about a minute, the little girl *was* his daughter, and by the time the medic on Rescue One took over breaths for him, he knew that his brain was just playing a particularly horrible joke on him.

The little girl that day hadn't been breathing when they pulled up, and she still hadn't been breathing when the ambulance screamed away toward the hospital. She never breathed again. Coin was the one who caught the mother in his arms when she came running down the street toward them, alerted by a neighbor that something was wrong. He was the one who'd held her as she kicked and beat and clawed at him. He put her in the engine with Tox's approval, normally something they never did, and he rode in the back with her, holding her like he was the seat belt that could keep her from this awful, unacceptable crash from which the woman would never recover.

And he knew for one moment—for those sixty seconds —what it would feel like to know his own daughter would never breathe again.

They'd dropped the mother off at the hospital. They'd

checked in with the rescue squad who were as shaken as the engine crew. They went to the grocery store and bought the steaks they'd forgotten to get in the morning shopping trip because that's what firefighters did. They just kept moving and doing what had to be done. If someone died on you in the morning, it didn't mean you automatically got to save the dead guy in the afternoon.

When they'd gotten back to the station, he hadn't told anyone what had happened to him. The way he'd seen his daughter instead of the patient—that was the kind of crap that got you kicked off the line if you weren't careful.

But Lexie had known in her usual Lexie way, and that night, when he'd gone down to take her a leftover brownie from a pan a citizen had dropped off, she'd said, "What happened?"

He had shrugged. "She died. It happens."

"No," she had said. "What happened to *you*?"

He'd told her, and if he was perfectly honest with himself, he could admit that he'd cried that night. She'd pretended not to notice, but she'd shoved the Kleenex box closer to him and had made a pot of coffee so he could collect himself. Then she'd told him to call Serena before he went to bed, something he didn't always do, and hadn't even thought about doing that night. It was such an obvious answer. It had just taken Lexie listening to him to get the answer he needed.

Now, as they drove toward the water, he said, "Sorry. I'm being awkward, huh?"

"Yeah," she said, keeping her gaze out her window. "But that's okay. I'm used to you being awkward."

He laughed. *I love you*, he wanted to say. He couldn't say it. But damn if he didn't want to.

CHAPTER 21

The cemetery. He'd taken her to the cemetery.

Lexie couldn't decide whether to be happy or to punch him in the arm. She settled on just saying, "I had no idea you were a vampire."

He reached into the bed of the truck and pulled out a black backpack. "Vampires don't hang out at cemeteries. Only ghouls do. And goths. I suppose they do, too."

Feeling for a moment as if she should dig in her heels, Lexie said, "Are you sure this is a good idea?"

Cheerfully, Coin said, "Nope."

"You're not?"

"Not even a little bit. But I'm hoping it's a good idea. I'm hoping it's a great one, actually." He turned to face her, and Lexie realized that even with the early fall evening around them, he filled her vision in a way she'd never noticed before. He seemed taller than the clear blue sky above them. A vineyard skated the edge of the cemetery and the yellow leaves of the grape vines echoed the color of the sycamore leaves. Far in the distance, over the rooftops of Darling Bay, the ocean sparkled blue and deep green.

And she couldn't take her eyes off Coin.

He smiled at her. "You can do this," said Coin. "Besides, I have something I want to show you."

"Don't take me there," said Lexie. She couldn't go to her father's grave. She hadn't been back since they'd buried him, not once.

"I won't. Not unless you want me to. I have something else to show you."

"This is officially the worst date I've ever been on in my life."

He smiled. "Just wait! It gets worse!"

Lexie reached forward and took the hand he offered. There was no way she was going to walk down those paths alone.

NIGHT DROPPED SLOWLY as they walked, turning the air a soft blue. The cemetery was enormous—something Lexie had forgotten. It was beautiful, she could admit that, especially in the golden fall sunset. Low rolling green hills were dotted with markers that went as far back as the early 1800s, something that wasn't common on a stretch of land so far west. The settlers who were buried here were the ones who'd fought their way to the coast, battling their way across mountains and deserts with a desire to see the Pacific and make a new home.

To the right, where Coin was leading them, were the crypts that resembled small, ornate houses made of marble. Some were from the turn of the last century, but Lexie could tell some were newer. Cleaner. People were still building homes for the afterlife, something that struck Lexie as both morbidly strange and eerily hopeful.

"Over here." Coin said. He gave her hand a squeeze, and for one moment Lexie imagined pulling on his hand, making him turn to hold her. She wanted Coins arms wrapped around her shoulders. If she could just bury her face in his jacket for a moment, maybe she wouldn't be feeling so lightheaded ... What if they accidentally walked past her father's grave? That day had been such a blur—she couldn't remember where on the grounds his stone was. What if she just glanced down and read the words *Robert Tindall*? She felt her hand go clammy in Coin's. Her stomach muscles contracted, and her footsteps slowed.

"Hey, now." Coin stopped. "You okay?" He looked carefully at her face. "We can go back if you want." He touched her shoulder.

Lexie gritted her teeth, sucking air around them. Then she said, "Is this going to be worth it?"

Coin touched her chin. "I'm taking you to see where my dad is, not yours."

His father? That was enough to shock her out of worrying about herself. He *hated* his father. It was the one thing Lexie had never been able to get him to tell her much about. "Why?"

"I just want you to see what he was like."

It was a good enough answer, for now at least. Lexie straightened her spine. "I'll follow you."

He hiked the backpack up his shoulder and nodded toward the green hillock on their right. "Almost there."

The crypt Coin led them to was one of the biggest crypts in the cemetery. It was in the shape of a pyramid, at least twenty feet high at its uppermost point. A path to the sealed door cut through the grass, and Coin went up the two steps to sit on the stoop in front of it. "I call this his front porch."

Lexie shaded her eyes against the last rays of the setting sun. To the west, the ocean sparkled a dark blue agate and a thin line of fog at the horizon stood at the ready. Overhead, two seagulls argued in an in-flight squabble.

She sat next to him. "The concrete is cold." It was, bone-chillingly so. Or was that just because she knew what was behind her? Her stomach was still so tight it almost hurt.

"I'm sorry, I meant to bring a blanket, but I forgot to put one in the truck."

"You usually bring a blanket on your dates? Is this something you do? Seduce women in the graveyard?" She kept her voice light.

He brushed his hair back as he opened the backpack. "This is a first."

Strangely, Lexie felt relieved. She was the only one he'd brought here. That was okay, then.

From the backpack, Coin pulled a bottle of red wine. "It's Forget Me Not's red zin from two years ago."

"Oh! Valentine's winery." Truck One's tillerman owned a small vineyard just up the coast that was his off-hours baby. "I liked that one. He gave me a bottle for Christmas."

Coin took out two plastic wine glasses and screwed on the stems. "Classy, right?"

"Mmm." Lexie looked again at the view. From here she thought she could just see the top of her house, if she was guessing the right color roof. For some reason, she couldn't picture her roof at all right now. She could picture Coin's dark eyes without looking his direction at all. But the color of the roof she'd lived under since she bought her house five years ago? She didn't have a clue.

"Here," he said. "Let's toast."

Lexie bit her bottom lip. "All right. On your father's grave, literally. What should we toast to?"

"Obviously, to health."

Lexie nodded. "L'chaim." She clinked her glass against his—really more like a plastic tap—and sipped. She kept her eyes on his, as one should do when toasting, and ignored the fact that her stomach went from knots to flips.

He really did have the sexiest bedroom eyes.

Which was an inappropriate line of thought to have while sitting on a tomb.

While Coin took food out of the backpack, she scooted backward so she could sit cross-legged. She touched the concrete at her knee with one finger. She cast her mind for something—anything—that she could say that might distract them from the awareness of where they were, but Coin didn't seem at all weirded out. He seemed relaxed, as if he hung out here all the time. And, heck, maybe he did.

"When was the last time you were here?"

Coin looked into the air as if calculating. "He died when I was twenty. I came back once with my mom before she died. So I guess it's been thirteen years or more."

She gaped. "You don't come here, either?"

"No reason to. I hated the guy."

It didn't make sense. If they both avoided the cemetery ... "Why are we *here?*"

"He was important to me."

"I thought you said ..."

"I said I hated him. That's true. But he's the reason I am who I am, and specifically, he's why I'm the father I am." Coin tore a piece of bread off the baguette and looked at it, as if he'd forgotten why he'd brought it.

Maybe this time he would tell her about it. "Talk to me."

Coin took a deep breath. "He was a horrible guy. Really, there was nothing good about him. Check this out," he said, gesturing at the crypt, his arms wide open. "Doesn't this look like somewhere you'd like to spend eternity?"

"Maybe," said Lexie, trying to be charitable. "If I were Egyptian, or wanted ... to stand out in California."

He snapped his fingers and then tapped the tip of his nose. "Bingo. He wanted to stand out. He always wanted the biggest. The best. He'd read about some actor who had a tomb built like this, something about it holding the life force inside, so he had this built when he could afford it. Of course, then he went and crashed his car, having left no life insurance for my mother. He had, however, bought half of this before he died, so they buried him, and then my mother went on paying for it for two years after he died. Charming, no?"

"Where is she?"

Coin laughed, but the tone of it was off. He wasn't amused. "He didn't want her near him. She had to buy her own plot, so she chose a spot next to her mother's grave in Birmingham. But just imagine that. A man who didn't want his own wife with him. Too stingy to make a place for her inside this behemoth. Wanted it all to himself."

"You're the opposite of him."

Coin took a taste of wine and then help up the plastic cup. "I hope so. Anyway, that reminds me." He took a smaller bottle out of the backpack. "Whiskey for the old man." He uncapped it and poured it at the base. "One for the homie. Oh, never mind, just have all of it, Dad. You always did." He paused. "You know, one time I made a list, thinking that if I listed all his bad qualities I might be able to remember a good one. I just wanted one. Know what I came up with?"

Lexie shook her head.

"He liked bacon. That was his best quality. Not that he cooked it well, or liked to make BLTs for the family. That would have been a good thing, and I couldn't find one of those. I just know that he liked bacon. To eat."

It clicked. "That's why you hate bacon."

"Yep."

"I just thought you were a bad person."

At that, Coin gave an unexpected hoot of laughter. "No. That's not why. Though by the way everyone talks about it, you'd think that was the case. It's just salted pork, people. Why is it such a big deal? I even hate the smell of it."

"I know." It was why, when they were on Sunday shift, Coin usually spent the morning in dispatch if there wasn't a call.

Well. She'd *thought* it was because of the bacon ...

Shaking her head to clear it, she said, "So now tell me how he was bad."

"Oh, you know. The usual way. He wasn't even an interesting kind of awful. He was a hitter. And a drinker. He liked to get loaded on cheap whiskey and knock my mom around."

Lexie winced.

"When I got tall enough to be in his way, he knocked me around the same way. I thought he was normal, though. I thought that dads hit and moms cried, and that was why I was never going to fall in love and have children, because I never wanted anyone to feel as scared as I did, listening to him whale on my mother."

"Oh, Coin."

He shrugged. "It was what I knew. Then I met Janice, and we got pregnant on accident. I thought my life was over, and I could just see myself going down that road. I think that's what pushed me and Janice apart—my fear that I would turn into him."

"That or the fact that she slept with the mailman."

He laughed again. "I still can't believe that. That she actually left me for Tom the mailman. But at least that was after we had Serena. When I saw my baby girl for the first time, I knew. I just knew I wouldn't be my father."

Lexie scooted an inch closer so that their knees were almost touching. More scarlet rays streaked across the darkening sky behind him. "How did you know?"

"Because I knew that no matter what, when my mother gave birth to me, he would never have held me the same way I held my baby daughter."

"How did you know? Did your mother tell you that?"

"I could feel it. If I'd ever been held by my dad like that, things would have been different. He wasn't supposed to be a father. I'm glad he was, naturally, because that means I'm here, drinking wine next to his old dead bones with the prettiest girl in the state. And I was. Meant to be a father, I mean. I knew that as soon as I got my arms around her."

Lexie set down her wine. She took his wine glass away and set it down.

"Hey, what—?"

"Hush," she said. "Just for a minute. I want to try something."

Then Lexie leaned forward and put her lips against his.

CHAPTER 22

Lexie told herself was really only a test to see if he still tasted as good as he had in his kitchen. It was a test to see if they would feel the same heat.

It wasn't the same. It was even hotter.

Coin initially seemed surprised, but it took him only a second to rev it up to super-heated, like she'd poured lighter fluid on a banked fire. He was with her, in the kiss, driving it. Twisting his body but not taking his mouth from hers, he pulled her into his lap so she lay across him. He smiled against her mouth and then nipped her bottom lip, eliciting a small gasp.

Lexie pulled back, suddenly worried. "Am I hurting you?"

"You? You're perfect. Right where you are."

"Are you sure?"

"Your body is perfect, Lex." He kissed her again, and for the first time in her adult life, Lexie didn't worry about her weight during a kiss. She didn't wonder if he could detect a roll at the top of her jeans, and she didn't worry whether her thighs were too wide. He'd pulled her into his lap like she didn't weigh an ounce, and she could feel the strength in his arms as they wrapped around her.

His mouth was hot, his tongue slick. She panted against him, and he gasped as she deepened the kiss. When she moved against him, she could feel his hardness, and a fevered thrill shot through her.

Lexie wanted more.

"Coin," she said against his mouth.

"Mmm?" He licked her top lip, sending another shiver down her spine.

"We're making out on your father's grave."

"Screw him."

"That's gross. And he's not the Keefe I want."

Coin pulled back. "I swear this wasn't the plan. We were just going to have a picnic, with wine and cheese and those double-stuffed Oreos you love."

"I started this," she said, trailing her fingers across his jawline, down his neck, tucking them under the neckline of his shirt. She wanted to touch more of him. All of him. "I want more."

Coin's dark eyes sparkled, even in the dark that was settling around them. "More of what?"

"More of you. More kisses. More skin." Lexie touched his belt buckle. "Less clothing."

"Where?"

"My house."

"Are you sure?"

Lexie considered for a moment. Did she want to take this man home? To her bed? It had been so long since she had a man stay the night that she couldn't remember the last time she'd brewed more than one cup of coffee in the morning. She didn't do this. She didn't take random men home with her.

But this wasn't just some guy she'd met.

It was Coin. Her best friend.

A week ago, she would have thought that would make it weirder. But it didn't.

It made it better.

"I'm sure. But before we go ... Can we ...?"

"You never ask for anything. Name it." His voice was rough. He meant it, she knew. He'd do anything for her.

"Before we go can we look for my father's grave?"

"You bet."

It turned out her father wasn't that far from Coin's. He was just over a small rise in what must have been a cheaper section. There were no crypts there, just modest markers, none more than two feet high.

"Here," said Coin.

Robert Tindall. It was clean, and well maintained. A bouquet of flowers stood at the foot of it, and a small American flag moved slowly in the autumn breeze.

"Oh," said Lexie. She had expected it would hurt to see it. That it would bring her to her knees. The reason she'd never gone to visit her father's grave was because she didn't want to cry again—ever—like she had when he died.

She'd never expected it would make her happy.

"Are you okay?"

"I'm fine." She laughed and tasted tears on her tongue. "I'm actually fine." She kneeled and touched the face of the stone. "Look. His name." Under it was chiseled a fire service crest, and the words "Darling Bay Fire Department, Lost in Action, Always Remembered."

"And the flowers." She touched the edge of a white rose and was surprised to notice her hand was shaking. "Look. They're real. Coin, they're fresh."

She turned to him. "Did you do this? Did you plan this?"

He held up his hands. "Not me, I swear. Is there a card with it?"

She explored at the base of the stems. "Yeah." Pulling it out, she knew by the handwriting even before she read the words. "My mom. It's from my mom."

"Well, that makes sense, doesn't it?"

Lexie sat back with a thump onto the grass. "No."

"Why not?"

"She never acts like she loved him."

"How?"

"She won't talk about him. She started dating six months after he died."

"Maybe she was lonely."

"What's wrong with *lonely* after your husband dies?"

"Everyone grieves in their own way."

"But not her. She barely grieved at all. You remember," said Lexie. It was suddenly incredibly important that he agree with her about this. "You remember, too. How it was."

Beloved by so many, the whole town had mourned the loss of Lexie's larger-than-life father. They'd actually hung black bunting—that hadn't been used since JFK—around Mabel's Cafe. City Hall had closed for the funeral. The fire department brought in engines from Eureka to cover the stations, and they'd borrowed a sheriff's dispatcher to work the ComCen. Lexie had heard later that the woman had been terrified she would have to dispatch a fire, but Darling Bay during Chief Tindall's funeral went completely silent, as if every single resident was grieving the loss. The worst thing Lexie had ever seen in her life was the line of fire trucks on First Street, their ladders up and stretched over the roadway, draped with giant flags, as she and her mother rode under them in the hearse from the church to the cemetery. And the men and women standing at attention in their Class As next to the rigs weren't just her father's employees to her. By then they were her coworkers. They were her friends. In a very real sense, her family.

Lexie could vividly remember Coin that day. He hadn't met her eyes when they'd driven by, he'd stayed at attention, his face strong. But she'd seen the tears dripping from his chin, darkening his shirt.

"You remember how it was," she said again.

"It was the worst loss Darling Bay Fire had ever had."

"My mother didn't act like the rest of the town. She didn't act like *strangers* did. She just moved on."

"Lexie, the last thing I want is to argue with you, but I know your mom. She loved him. Take it from someone whose parents didn't have that together. She still loves him."

"The last man she dated updated maps for the road service. A more boring man could never exist even if you cloned him and gave him a robot soul."

"Huh," said Coin, brushing off the top of the stone with his hand.

"What?"

"Seems to me like maybe that's why she dated him."

The thought was new, and somehow frightening. Could it be true that both she and Mira stayed away from men with high risk jobs because they were still too sad to risk their hearts? Lexie knew that's what it was for her, even though she hated to admit it. But maybe that's how her mother loved her father, too? Mira hadn't dated a single man who had any characteristic in common with Robert Tindall, in either looks or personality. Every man she'd gone out with had been white collar with day jobs. She'd dated a banker, two lawyers, and an accountant. "Every single one of them was boring," she said softly.

"What?"

"Oh, I'm just thinking ... you're right."

Coin smiled. "Can I get you on record saying that?"

"No, really. All of them have been boring. And I've been so *mad* at her this whole time."

"But ..."

"But she's been dating the exact opposite of Dad."

"What does the note say?"

Lexie's eyes widened. "I can't look."

"Too private. I get it."

"No, it's just that *I* can't do it. Too weird. Will you read it for me?"

"You sure?"

Lexie nodded. She bit the inside of her lip hard, and for a moment the blood tasted like tears, too.

Coin squatted and opened the small, folded card. "It just says 'Always.'"

A yellow bloom of pain glared against the back of Lexie's eyelids, as if a flashbulb had gone off. And maybe one had, because it was clear now. *Always.* Lexie was side-swiped with a memory—when she was very young, she'd asked her mother why he said it instead of "goodbye," like the other fathers did. "Because he wants to make sure that if he doesn't make it home, that it was his last word to me." When she'd asked why her father might not come home, she hadn't understood why her mother just shook her head. Lexie was too young then to realize that not all firefighters did.

She stood, holding out her hand for her best friend to take. "Take me home, please," said Lexie.

Coin broke the speed limit on the way to her house.

Lexie found an old receipt in the truck's door pocket and folded into a tiny square, over and over again, trying to ignore how anxious her stomach felt.

At home, as she fumbled with fingers made thick from excitement to get the front door unlocked, he asked, "Do you really want this?"

"Yes."

"Lexie. We can still go backward. But if we go forward, I'm not going to be able to get over you. Do you understand that?"

In answer, she kissed him. "Forward," she said against his mouth. "I want forward."

In her head she heard the word she wanted to say, *Always*. She couldn't say it. But she heard it.

CHAPTER 23

Coin was used to waking up in strange beds.

At the station, they all had preferred dorm beds, but if you worked a shift with a guy on overtime who had more seniority and liked your bunk, you got booted to your second- or third-favorite. So when he opened his eyes to find himself looking at a bookshelf, he just blinked.

But he wasn't at the station. There was no air filter running at high volume, no sound of early risers working out in the engine bay.

He wasn't at home.

The wall behind the bookcase was yellow.

Lexie's favorite color.

He grinned, memories from the night before flooding his mind. The look of her, underneath him, soft and warm and perfectly everything he'd ever imagined and a whole hell of a lot more. Her eyes when he made love to her. The way they'd clung to each other afterward, as if they'd both found exactly where they needed to be.

She'd fit into his arms like she'd come home, and Coin

had wanted to stay there forever in the dark, his arms wrapped around her, keeping her safe.

He rolled over, wanting to see her, to touch her. She'd be there, sweet and gorgeous, and he'd kiss her again. And again. There was nothing in the whole wide world like kissing Lexie. He didn't want to do anything else, ever.

But she wasn't there. Her pillow was cool but her spot under the covers was still warm, so she couldn't have gone far. He sat up, smelling coffee.

Coin helped himself to a mug and found Lexie on the front porch, wrapped in a yellow terry robe. Instead of sitting on the porch swing, she sat on the top step, as if waiting for someone. When the screen door closed behind him, she didn't turn around.

"Good morning, darlin'," he said.

She didn't answer. Her shoulders were hunched, as if she was in pain.

"What's wrong?" He set the mug on the rail and sat next to her.

She just shook her head. Her hair was a mess of red curls and her eyes had the shadows under them she got when she couldn't sleep.

"Tell me, Lex."

"You just called me Darling."

"Darlin'. It's very different."

"That's my work name. That's how we go on the radio. Every firefighter calls me that all day. I can't ..."

A cold shard of fear pierced him. "You can tell me. You can tell me anything, you know that."

"No, I mean I can't do this."

It was like a gut punch. Coin pulled back. "Excuse me?"

"Us. I can't do this."

"We *did* do this. I thought ... last night ..."

"Was a mistake."

Confusion filled him. He took a sip of coffee but it was bitter in his mouth. "Lexie, we talked about it. What changed?"

She covered her face with her hands, and stayed quiet.

Old Mrs. Finch walked past with Clancy, her Great Dane who was almost as tall as she was. Coin nodded in response to her surprised "Oh!"

Lexie glanced at him, her eyes full of tears.

"Lex. Tell me. Tell me all of it."

She shook her head. "I don't want to do this to you."

"What can't you do?"

Turning to face him, she said, "Don't make us do this."

"We don't have to do anything we don't want to." Where had this come from? She'd gone to sleep almost purring in his arms.

"It can't work."

"Why not?"

"Because you're in love with me."

It was true. Coin figured probably every guy in the station and certainly every woman knew it. Hank had told him outright that he knew. Tox had told him, too. Coin protested out loud at every opportunity. But now? He wouldn't protest. He'd hire a skywriter to tell everyone. "I am."

"See, that's—"

"And you're in love with me."

Her mouth fell open. "What?"

"You're in love with me, too." Coin knew it, suddenly. He knew it in his bones. He'd felt it before, a million times. The way they laughed together all night in the ComCen, the way they tended to gravitate toward each other all day in the station, as if they were stuck in orbit around each other. The way her eyes lit when she saw him. She didn't look that way at anyone else.

But more than that, he'd felt it last night when he'd held her.

And he felt it now, even though she looked more surprised than if he'd given her a pony. "Tell me you're not."

She started to speak, her face confident. "I'm ..."

He leaned against the porch rail and took a sip of his coffee.

"I'm ..."

"Go ahead, say it," he encouraged.

Her eyes flashed. "Don't you dare tease me. I hate you."

"And ..." He moved his hand in a go-ahead motion. "And you ..."

"I love you," she snapped. "Of course I do. I love all my guys. I don't date them. Any of them. Ever. But I love my firefighters."

"That's where you're wrong," Coin said easily, sure of nothing more. "You're in love with me."

Instead of looking happy about it, she looked stricken. "Oh, damn," she said. "I am."

CHAPTER 24

It was true. He was right. The knowledge landed on top of Lexie's head like a load of wet laundry, heavy and cold.

She couldn't be in love with him. She just couldn't.

Next to her, Coin laughed, a round, joyful sound. "Isn't that a good thing?"

"No."

"Lexie?" He touched her shoulder but she shrugged him off and stood.

"You have to go."

"Darlin'."

"Don't *call* me that. Look, you've always said you'll do anything for me, right?"

He nodded. His eyes held a look that Lexie couldn't bear to see. "Anything. Name it, Lexie, and I'll do it."

"Then go." She paused, locking her hands in front of her as if that could protect the heart she hadn't even known she'd lost. "Don't ask me anything else, not for one other single thing. I've already told you the truth, that should be enough for you. Do you have your keys?"

He nodded.

"Just go."

"That's what you want from me? That's truly what you want?"

"And don't come back. Not like this. We can't do this. Friends, Coin, that's what we are. At work, we'll be friends, just like always." Her voice thinned and she pictured for a moment Coin casually bringing her coffee in the morning, telling her about the date he'd gone on the night before. She heard, rather than felt, her heart start to break. "That's all we can ever be. I can't love a firefighter, Coin. I can't lose another one. In the middle of the night I still hear them yelling." She meant the firefighters who had come up screaming that night her father died, and she knew he understood that. "I promised myself."

Coin grimaced and rubbed the side of his jaw, where the stubble was growing in thick. Just an hour ago, she'd been pressed tight against him, kissing him right there while he slept. She knew how sharp the stubble felt against her lips, and for a second, she wished they could be back in bed again, back to the time before she realized she'd screwed it all up.

"Do you know what you're asking me to do?"

She didn't look at him. She couldn't. She only nodded.

"Are you sure?" His voice was rough. She heard heartbreak under the words and felt her own heart shatter to match his.

"It's what I want. It's what I need." And without waiting to watch him leave, Lexie went into the house. She shut the door behind her and leaned, her palms flat against the wood.

Last night, he'd carried her in the house as if she hadn't weighed a thing. She'd loved that, that he could toss her around like she were a bag of groceries. Later, he'd carried her to bed, where he proceeded to have his talented way with her. In the past she'd dated men she was terrified she might break, skinnier than she was with lightweight limbs. She'd never been a fan of having to be careful like that. Last night, Coin had given as much as she had. Where she nipped, he bit back. He'd pinned her arms over her head, and she'd wrapped her legs around him, not letting him go. Then, when they'd held each other to sleep, she'd felt supported. Safe.

Coin always made her feel like that. He'd always made her feel safe, she realized. It was a lie—he was the most unsafe thing in her entire life.

Her phone rang. It was either Coin wanting to come back, or her mother, the only person who ever called her at this hour. She looked at her phone. Coin's number wasn't displayed.

"How did your *date* go?" trilled her mother.

She knew, goodness only knew how. Darling Bay was small, but it had an incredibly high big-mouth-per-capita. At times, Lexie had enjoyed this. Right then, it wasn't the town's best feature.

"What are you trying to ask, Mom?"

"Coin Keefe? Really, Lexington?"

Lexie groaned and slid sideways so she was lying on the couch, her feet propped on the armrest. "So?"

"So. He's got a child."

"He does. Serena's awesome."

"He was married!"

"He's not now. That's the important part, right?"

"I don't trust those eyes of his."

"How well do you know his eyes, Mom?"

"He was at your Christmas party last year. He told me he was thinking of getting a motorcycle."

"And he did." Lexie had ridden on the back of it once in the station's parking lot. Now she looked back at that moment and realized that yes, maybe she had enjoyed that a little too much. As if it were yesterday, she could remember the breadth of his back against her chest, and the feeling of resting her hands at his waist. Why didn't she know then? Why did this come as such a surprise?

"I always said don't ever date a man with a motorcycle. The mortality factor is too high."

"I'm a fire and medical dispatcher, Mother. I'm aware of the fatality rate—not the mortality factor—and I'm not worried about it because I'm not dating him."

"Why was he at your house this morning?"

"Having coffee."

"At seven in the morning?"

"Do you have a *camera* on my house?"

"Mrs. Finch told Mabel Mellor who sent me an email."

Lexie glanced at the wall clock. Less than ten minutes. That's how long it took gossip to get to her mother in this town. "Well, he's not here now."

"Did I tell you about my friend, Marge Bondy?"

Lexie sighed. No matter what, a story that started with "did I tell you about" never ended well with her mother. "No."

"I met her on Facebook in a widow's group, but she's a good friend now. Her husband was a firefighter."

"And he perished horribly in flames," said Lexie tightly. "I get it."

"Don't jump to conclusions. It's not polite. Her husband died in his sleep of a massive heart attack."

"Brought on by the stress of being a firefighter?"

"Stop it. No, I don't think they thought that's what caused it. He was unhealthy anyway. Diabetes in his last years."

Lexie felt mild chagrin. "Oh. Sorry. What about her?"

"Her *daughter* died," said her mother triumphantly. "She was a firefighter, too. While she was on scene of a freeway accident, a car hit her as it passed by. Knocked her right out of her work boots."

She should have known. "Got it, Mom."

"I'm serious. Don't date a firefighter."

Lexie rubbed the tension that had suddenly built up in her shoulders. "I said I got it. I won't."

"You won't? Really?" Her mother's voice was two shades lighter.

"He doesn't mean anything to me," Lexie said. Her throat ached.

"Oh, thank goodness. Now, I have to ask you. How do you feel about florists? Because I met a man named Kenneth who said he has a son he's desperate to get out of his house."

CHAPTER 25

The first call of the day was from PD, a drunk guy in the bushes. Coin was the one lucky enough to find him, and doubly lucky to be the one the guy chose to vomit on while they were taking vitals.

The second call was for a rattler in a back yard. Usually animal control would handle it, but they were closed, and the people in the house were having a birthday party that afternoon, so Tox killed the snake and then Coin drew the short straw to dispose of the body. Hank just laughed when they got back in the rig. "Puke and rattlesnake blood, two liquids we never thought we were signing up to handle, huh?"

The next call—Lexie gave it to them even though they'd requested to return to the station for cleanup—was to change the batteries in an old lady's smoke detector that she couldn't reach.

"I'm not going in," said Coin, hitting the brakes too hard in front of the battery house. "I'm filthy, and if I go in there, the woman will probably dump battery acid in my lap or something. I'm staying out here."

"I'll stay with you," Hank said cheerfully.

But Tox, their captain, said, "You're coming with me. You think I don't know that Samantha lives next door?"

"And saying hello to her would be ... wrong?" Hank had been hovering around Samantha Rowe for months now.

Tox said, "If I have to change a stupid battery, then I need backup, and Coin stinks too bad."

Coin sighed and rested his head on the steering wheel. It was already the worst day ever, and it just kept getting better. Every time Lexie spoke on the radio, he felt ill.

Coin had screwed it all up by moving too fast.

He shouldn't have pushed her to admit she was in love with him—*he'd* known it was true, but it seemed as if she hadn't. The realization had been a shock to her system, and it hadn't seemed like a good one.

And then should have stayed. He should have planted himself firmly on her porch and refused to leave. But the whole point was that she never asked him to do a thing, and that he'd always said he would do anything for her. What he'd meant by that was that he'd take a bullet for her. Step in front of a train. Drag her prized possession out of a four-alarm fire.

Take her to Bora Bora.

Not leave. The first thing she'd ever asked him for was for him to leave. He couldn't have said no. But by acceding to her wish, Coin knew he'd lost her forever. By now she'd probably talked herself out of feeling anything for him. He'd seen her do it before. When her dad died, she'd refused to talk to anyone, saying she was fine. She'd maintained that party line until HR believed her and let her come back. But he'd seen her that first week back on the job. She had literally white-knuckled it. Whenever anyone was looking at her she seemed like her good old Lexie self, laughing and joking with the guys and with the other dispatchers. He'd overheard her manager tell Lexie that she shouldn't handle the next fire. Someone else could do it. That very night they'd gotten a good one-alarm room-and-contents fire, and Lexie hadn't given up control. She'd handled the radio as she had every one of her other fires—like a pro.

But one time, that first week she was back, he'd been working outside the dispatch window trimming the hydrangeas that grew in their large planter. He'd looked in and had caught sight of her, her fingers wrapped through and around her headset cord as if knitting it between her hands. Her face had been stark white, her lips pale. Her eyes had held the unshed tears it had probably taken all her strength to hold back.

Even then, years ago, he'd wanted to go inside and ease her pain.

The only thing she'd ever wanted from him was for him to leave.

Coin groaned and got out of the rig. He needed to move, to stretch his legs. If he stood in front of the engine, he'd be able to see the wharf from here. Maybe that would help. He doubted it. Really, the only thing that had helped was Serena this morning at her mom's when he'd dropped off a book she needed. She'd hugged him hard and said, "Don't look so sad. If you can't fix a problem, you're not trying hard enough."

This he didn't know if he could fix. Yeah, he would try his hardest, but besides being the love of his life, Lexie was also the most stubborn woman he'd ever met. She didn't change her mind quickly or easily. Ever.

He sat on the rig's fender. Below, the road wound into town, and over the tops of the roofs came the sound of barking seals and the metal dings of sail lines hitting masts. Another gorgeous day in paradise.

No wonder he felt like hell.

"Hey, buddy, can you help me?"

To his right, a short man with a shaved head wearing an old black T-shirt and jeans that had seen better days, shuffled forward, his hand extended. His fingers were as dirty as his face.

Darling Bay had two homeless guys, both named Pete. The Petes were harmless, and the Darling Bay council let them have a key to the city garage in the winter so they'd stay dry. When firefighters went to pump gas, either the younger or the older Pete would help, washing as far up a window as he could reach, which was never far. They were cheerful, harmless fellows who knew everyone.

Coin didn't recognize this man, and something about his eyes made him stand up off the bumper. "What do you need help with?"

"I just got this thing, I need you to check it out."

Fabulous. He'd probably get a closeup view of the guy's junk in a minute and have to street-diagnose some rash. Maybe the guy would pee on Coin's shoe, then his day would be completely perfect. He looked over the man's shoulder toward the house but neither Tox nor Hank had come back out yet. How long did it take to change a dang battery? She was probably one of those who said "a battery for my smoke detector" but actually meant "I'm lonely, please fix my screen door and my dryer while you're here." They got their fair share of those calls.

"Sorry, buddy, but whatever it is, I can't make a diagnosis out here. I'm not a doctor. Do you need an ambulance to take you to the hospital?"

"Nah," the man said, "I need your morphine."
Too late, Coin saw the gun.

CHAPTER 26

Lexie'd had been a horrible day. The first thing Megan had said was, "How'd it go with Coin?"

Lexie had burst into tears.

Lexie didn't cry in dispatch. Really, she tried to cry nowhere at all, but crying in dispatch was against all her work rules, every single one. If you told a woman how to do CPR on her husband—a man she couldn't lose, a man she told over and over as she pumped, "Please don't leave me, love. Please don't leave me, love"—you just hung up the phone at the end of the call and kept on with whatever you'd been doing before the phone rang. Emailing reports. Making a sandwich. Gossiping with a coworker. You did *not* cry.

So when Lexie broke into sobs at Megan's question, she had no idea what to do. Megan looked as horrified as Lexie felt. "Oh, honey. Oh, no. Oh, what can I do?"

At every *Oh*, Lexie wanted to howl louder, but she managed to bring it down. She sniffled her way through six Kleenex, finally biting her inner lip hard enough to draw blood which at least made her stop blubbering like an idiot.

"I'm fine. I'll be fine."

Thankfully, 911 rang and Megan had thrown her body at the phone like she was covering a live grenade. By the time Megan hung up with the caller, Lexie had dried her eyes completely. She then distracted her with the speculation that one of the keyboards was dying, and they'd moved on. Megan hadn't asked her another word.

The calls were rough, too. One unsuccessful suicide attempt, two possible strokes, one elderly fall victim who'd been down all night, unable to get to the phone. At least she got to make sure Engine One stayed out of the station. Lexie felt incrementally better when she could double click on its automatic vehicle locator and make sure she wasn't going to accidentally run into Coin in the hallway or the kitchen, because he was out working in his zone. Good grief, if she couldn't control her emotions when Megan simply asked her a question, how would she control herself when she actually saw the man?

She *missed* him.

That was possibly the worst part. Funny how she'd never noticed before that every day started with him. She bet Coin knew it. Even on her off-duty days, she usually woke to a text. Coin would send her Serena's latest not-funny joke, or ask her how many lemons he should put in lemonade. Something. There was always something on her phone from him when she woke at home. At work, he brought her coffee. Every morning.

She missed him so much. His voice, his laugh, the way he looked at her like she was something special, someone beautiful.

This morning, he hadn't come in.

Lexie thought she might have been okay if he had. Like

after her father died, she'd push the emotion into a compart-
ment and deal with it another day. Or never.

He hadn't brought her coffee, though. She looked him
up in Telestaff to see if he'd called out sick or been moved to
a different station for the day. Nope. There was his name,
big as life, on Engine One, right where he normally was.
The taste of disappoint had warred with abject relief. Fine,
he was ignoring her. She could do the same until she healed.
Until she got over him.

Considering that she'd just found out she was *into* him,
she had no idea how long that would be. When she'd
grabbed extra creamer from the kitchen, she'd heard his
laugh in the apparatus bay. If she'd been asked on 911 if a
heart could physically twist inside a chest, she'd have been
pretty confident that it couldn't. But hers was starting to
make a habit of it.

She knew she shouldn't have sent them on the battery-
change call. Normally that was something they held for a
free crew. It definitely wasn't something they'd give to a
crew who needed to come in for cleanup. One of them was
either covered in vomit or rattlesnake juice, or both, and by
now Tox and Hank probably hated her right along with
Coin.

Lexie wondered what Coin had told the guys about her.
She stuck a Tootsie Pop into her mouth and didn't, for a
moment, notice that she'd forgotten to take the paper off.

She just couldn't let him come back to the station yet.
She needed another ten minutes. Maybe another ten
minutes after that, too. Maybe she could make Engine One
stay out till her afternoon rest period. She'd eat dinner in
dispatch instead of grabbing it down the hall, and if he did
come in, she'd fake a headache.

He wasn't coming in, though. She knew that. If Coin

had been going to come try to change her mind, he would have already done it.

The fact that he hadn't meant he'd changed his mind about her.

How could a heart that had barely learned it was in love break with such a shattering smash?

The radio squawked, drawing her attention away from the window and the two skateboarding kids in front, back to her screen.

"Last unit?" she asked.

No answer.

"Was there a unit with traffic for Darling?"

Still no answer.

Fine. So it was open air, someone hitting their side mike with their butt as they got in a rig. She wondered if it was Coin, if it came from his mike. Was he possibly thinking about her right now, too? Or was he up a ladder inside, changing batteries?

What if he'd fallen?

It was a silly fear, and she felt ashamed as soon as she'd had it. Coin was fine. If he'd fallen, the first thing Tox would have done would be to call on the radio for a rescue ambulance.

Another squawk.

No. Something was wrong. Lexie heard something in the background that was off. She couldn't have described it for anyone else, and she wished Megan were in the room to ask her if she'd gotten the same gut feeling from the sound of the open air.

"Last unit, go again."

The emergency beacon flashed on her screen. It was labeled Engine One.

"Engine One, are you clear for a code three hundred?"

There was a pause, and then Coin's voice came back, clear as day and calm as he'd ever sounded, "Affirm. I'm clear."

The innocuous words were code. They meant the opposite. They meant he was in serious trouble.

Lexie said with an equal calm she didn't feel in her heart, "Copy that."

And she sprang into action.

CHAPTER 27

"See, man? I told the dispatcher I was okay. That's what code three hundred means. She was just checking on me. They have to do that. What's your name, anyway?"

"I don't gotta tell you. Just give me the stuff. Hurry up."

They were in the rig, the man in the front passenger seat where Tox usually sat. "I just want to know your first name. You don't have to tell me your last name. I'm Coin."

"What kind of a name is that?"

"My dad liked money. What's yours?"

"Louis." The man looked chagrined, and the pistol drooped in his hand. "But they call me Trigger."

That wasn't a soothing thing to hear.

"Okay, Louis. Here's what I'm concerned about."

"No concerns! Just give me what you have."

"We don't have—"

"Now!" Louis was getting more agitated by the minute. "Just give it to me."

Over Louis's shoulder, he saw Hank and Tox run out the front door of the house. They froze on the lawn when they saw someone else in the engine with Coin. They knew as well as anyone else in the department what a code three hundred meant, even if none of them had ever heard a real one before.

Coin dragged his eyes away from them before Louis noticed.

"That's what I'm trying to tell you. We don't carry drugs on the engine. Only the rescue ambulance has those."

Louis looked confused.

"I'm telling you the truth. I couldn't give you anything if I wanted to. And I do want to, Louis. You're obviously upset—"

"You're lying!"

"But before you do something you'll regret, before you do something you can't take back, I suggest you jump down and take off running."

"Where's the ambulance, then?" Louis looked out the window as if he could make one appear. "Get one here."

"Come on, buddy. You think I can just call an ambulance and get it here?"

"If I have a gun in your face, you can't do that? To save your own life you're not gonna do that?"

Sirens wailed in the distance.

"What's that? Why are they coming?"

Coin held up his hands, careful to move slowly. "I don't know. But what I think you should do is get out of here as fast as you can. You can still get away."

"Not without what I came for. Use that thing." He pointed at the radio. "Get the ambulance here."

Coin's heart froze. What if this guy was really serious? What if he didn't care how many people he took out on the way to get his fix?

What about Lexie? She'd never know that he'd really

meant it—she'd never know that she was his heart, his every-thing. His love.

"Okay, Louis. I'll call an ambulance." He let Louis think he was doing it for him.

It wasn't totally true. He knew how this would probably play out. Coin was calling it for himself.

CHAPTER 28

W hen Coin called the code three hundred, Lexie turned into a blur of action. Her heart might have been beating a thousand times faster than normal, but that was nothing she hadn't worked around before. She paged Megan up from her rest, and she called in Sue, who lived two blocks away. She called PD and had them head toward Coin's location, code three. She started two engines, two rescues, and Jack Barger, the battalion chief on duty. She started a helo, staging it on the football field at the high school, two blocks away from the call.

In between this, the phone rang off the hook—every current chief, every retired chief, every curious and worried member of the department wanted to know what was going on. Lexie and Megan slapped them all on perma-hold. Every minute on the phone was a minute she could miss a transmission from Coin. They could rot before she answered their idiotic questions.

Her heart.

"Darling Fire, are you reporting an emergency?" she

said as quickly as she could to the next caller, her finger already hovering over the Hold button.

"Lex, it's Tox. He's with a guy with a gun in the engine."

"Is he hurt?"

"We don't think so."

"Suspect description?" Lexie snapped her fingers at Megan to get her attention. Without being asked, Megan dialed PD back to give them the update Lexie was typing into the call.

"White male, maybe forty-five, wearing a black T-shirt. That's all I can see from the porch. He yelled out the window at us to stay back."

"What kind of gun?" Lexie typed as fast as Tox talked.

"Black handgun, maybe semiautomatic."

"Anyone else around? On foot? Other cars?"

"Nothing evident."

The radio blurted its open mike sound, and Lexie threw Tox on hold without saying anything.

She waited. Megan hung up with the police dispatcher and stayed silent in her chair, her fingers over the keyboard, listening as hard as Lexie was.

"Darling Fire, Engine One calling."

Lexie took half a breath to still her vocal chords and then said as evenly as she could, "Go ahead to Darling."

"Can you start a rescue my direction?"

Megan gasped.

Lexie said with a confidence she didn't feel, "Affirm, Engine One. Reason?"

There was a pause, and Lexie wondered if it was possible to actually die from fear.

Finally Coin said, "Well, number one, I got a guy

named Louis with me here. He needs a fix of something and I think we'll give it to him, okay, Darling?"

"Affirm," Lexie managed.

"And number two," Coin continued, his voice steady over the air in her headset. "I have to tell you something, Darling Fire."

"Go ahead."

"I love you, darlin'. I always have. I love you more than anyone except Serena, and you tell her I said so, that's what I need you to do for me, and know that I love—"

A thunderclap filled her ears, and the radio went silent.

Four firefighters entered dispatch at a run, their faces drawn. Mazanti made sure the door shut with barely a click, and none of them made a sound. Even the phones stopped ringing.

Lexie only knew one thing—she needed to be with him. The only thing that kept her in her chair was the fact that she didn't trust anyone else to be on the radio right now. She couldn't lose him this way. The same way.

She couldn't.

The radio blared into activity. Tox yelled, "Get the rescue here, Darling! Code three!"

As if she'd send the ambulance in any other way. As if they'd *respond* any other way. Lexie knew the crew on Rescue Two were almost as panicked as she was.

They weren't in love with Coin, though. He was their friend, but not their best friend.

Coin was her love. Coin was *hers*. Other radios blared, stepping on each other's traffic.

"Units, *clear the air*." It was Lexie's radio now. "Captain One, status check," she said.

Tox responded, "He's hit, Darling. In the chest. We got vitals, but his heart rate's slipping."

"Battalion One, copy?" She released the pedal and coughed, the sob she wouldn't release becoming a physical thing in her chest.

"Affirm," shouted Chief Barger, his siren blaring in the background.

Lexie coughed, trying to clear her throat.

Megan said, "Can I take the radio for you?"

Lexie just shook her head, hard. This was hers. She would do her job. Maybe if she did her job the best she could, *this* time she could save the man she loved. She had to. With the sleeve of her sweatshirt, in between transmissions, she wiped the tears that dripped off her cheek. Every other second, she typed as fast as she could.

She did her job.

CHAPTER 29

Coin woke up in pain.

Pain everywhere. From the front of his forehead all the way to his kneecaps, as if his body was on fire. The worst was when he tried to breathe—it felt as if a ladder had been propped on his chest and the biggest guys in the department—Tox, Devo, Stu—were climbing it.

He knew he wasn't in the dorm. He wasn't in his own house. And with the beeping and white wall and blue curtain, he sure as heck wasn't at Lexie's.

The hospital.

He couldn't remember a dang thing, though.

Sleepy. He was so tired ...

But no, this was important.

If he was in the hospital, then something had happened. A fire—was that why his lungs hurt? He couldn't remember ...

It was quiet in this room with just the low beep of his heart monitor punctuating his thoughts. In the hall he heard voices, but their words didn't make sense.

Had he had a stroke? That wouldn't explain the pain.

Walk it back, Keefe.

He'd been at work. It had been a bad day.

Coin wracked his brain. *Why* had it been a bad day? Serena? His heart rate sped up—it was amplified by the electronic beeps. Was she okay? Had something happened, a car accident?

A nurse entered carrying a syringe.

"What happened? My daughter—"

"You're awake!" The nurse, an older woman with graying hair pulled back in a short ponytail, had young eyes. "Your daughter will be so pleased."

Relief flooded his body, pure and clean. For a second nothing hurt at all.

Lexie. Another pulse of adrenaline went though him. What wasn't he remembering? Something about Lexie. He remembered the kiss in the cemetery, and then the night they'd spent together came back to him.

It was a wonderful memory. It was perfect. Why then, did he ...

Oh.

He remembered. All of it, it came back in the space of a few seconds. The junkie with the gun, the way he'd aimed, and then fired.

What he'd told Lexie on the radio.

What Lexie had asked him to do—to leave her. To not come back.

"Where was I hit?" Coin croaked, trying to keep the despair from filling him completely, from drowning him.

"Eleven millimeters from your heart. If the man's hand had shaken even the tiniest bit, you wouldn't be here right now."

If he wasn't here, it wouldn't hurt this bad, knowing he'd tried to win her, and lost. But that wasn't fair—that wasn't right. He couldn't think that. The most important thing to think about was Serena. He had to get better for her.

"I'm going to call your daughter," said the nurse. "She's with her mother in the waiting room. They've refused to leave." She hung another liter of fluids. "You should also know that at any given point, there are at least six firefighters out there, sometimes more. I don't think there's been a time that room has been empty."

"How long ...?"

"Not that long, hon." She glanced at her watch. "You've been here for about twenty-three hours. You had surgery yesterday and you got moved out of recovery six hours ago. I have to say, it's heartening to see the way your coworkers care about you. And your wife! How on earth do you work with your wife? I couldn't work at this hospital if my Bernie worked here. I'd stab him with a pencil before the first day was out, but that said, he'd probably like it. I'll go get them now."

Coin tried to shake his head to clear it, but it hurt too much. He gasped and stilled. What did the nurse mean? He didn't work with Janice. Nothing made sense. All he knew was that he wanted to see Serena, wanted to hug her, to make sure she was okay.

And he wanted to see Lexie.

Not that it would happen. He tried, he'd failed.

Somehow he would have to find a way to be okay with being just friends with her. He couldn't imagine it—being with her in dispatch and not noticing the way the sun came through the window, lighting up those red curls. Sitting next to her while they did the crossword and not being distracted by the light scent of that flowery hand lotion she liked. Knowing how far that rose tattoo went and not getting to caress it again. Hearing her speak, watching her mouth move without wanting to kiss her.

He released a painful breath and closed his eyes. *That* was why his chest ached so much. Not the bullet wound. It was the broken heart that hurt the most.

For Serena, he was glad he'd lived. But she was the only reason he had any gladness at all.

"Daddy!"

Coin's eyes flew open and he smiled at the sight of his daughter, her hair taken out of her usual messy pigtails and combed neatly. "Come here, kiddo."

She looked as if she was almost overcome with the effort of not moving, her eyes blinking faster than normal. "I can't hug you. They said."

"I don't care what they said. I won't heal without a hug. You can fix me."

"Daddy," she laughed. "No, I can't. I'm not a wizard."

"If you can't fix it," he started.

"I'm not trying hard enough," Serena finished. Carefully, she leaned forward and gave him a sideways half-hug. It was enough. It was exactly what Coin needed.

"I can tell I'm already better. You think I should get up?"

"No!" Serena grinned. "No way."

"I love you, kid."

She shrugged. "I know."

"Where's your mom?"

"At home."

He frowned. "Oh. The nurse said ... Wait, your mom left you alone in the waiting room?"

"Seriously? There's like eleven hundred million firefighters out there playing poker. I already made fifteen bucks. Mom left me with Lexie."

Maybe they'd left something in his chest, because it suddenly felt as if Coin couldn't breathe. "Lexie's out there?"

"No," came a voice at the door. "I'm here."

CHAPTER 30

Lexie wanted more than anything to go to him like Serena had, to lean over and kiss him. To touch him. Her fingers itched to reach for him, to smooth the line between his eyes, to touch the stubble that had grown dark and thick over the last twenty-four hours.

But it wasn't that easy.

"Hi," she said.

"Hi, you." His voice was scratchy, as if it hurt to use.

"You look like crap," she said.

"Thanks. So do you."

Lexie laughed, surprised at how easy it was. To be here. She pushed her hair off her face. "Yeah, well. I haven't slept in a day and a half."

Coin took his daughter's hand. "Serena, honey?"

Serena rolled her eyes. "I'm not *stupid*. But be quick about it. I want to show you my favorite new card trick. Hank taught me." She ran out the door, whistling.

Lexie said, "Don't worry, I made sure he didn't use the naked lady deck."

Coin laughed, but his face went white.

Extending her hand, Lexie gripped the rail on his bed. "No, don't laugh. You should sleep. I should let you sleep more. You just woke up ..." She turned, flustered, but Coin's hand on her wrist stopped her.

"You're here."

"Of course I am. We're friends. Where else would I be?"

A light went out in his eyes, a light Lexie didn't know was so important to her.

"Call me darlin'," she said, surprising herself.

"What?"

She shook her head. "Just do it."

"Darlin'."

Lexie's hands started to shake.

"Darlin'," he said again, and there it was, the light was coming back.

She clenched her fingers into fists, but the trembling got worse.

"You know what, darlin'?"

She shook her head.

"I didn't know if I'd ever get to call you that again."

"You probably say that to all the dispatchers." She was glad her voice didn't quaver like the rest of her body had decided to do. What if he didn't remember anything? Any of it?

"Only the ones I love."

She opened her mouth but couldn't find the words she needed.

"Only the ones I'm in love with."

Lexie gave a strangled laugh. "I sent you away."

"I was going to honor that, I swear I was. It's just that, when I was in the rig with that guy—Louis—I could see in his eyes he wasn't going anywhere if he didn't get his fix, and he was going to take someone with him."

Coin's eyes asked the question he didn't voice. Lexie said, "He was a better shot with the bullet he put into himself. He didn't make it."

He said, "Yeah. I figured that. And I knew that I couldn't leave this big old world that I love so much without telling you and Serena one more time that I loved you."

Lexie reached for his hand. "Will I hurt you if ...?"

"Nothing you can do can hurt me."

Oh, she wasn't sure about that. If he felt one tenth of the emotion that she held in her heart right then, then she could hurt the hell out of him with a few well-chosen words.

So Lexie chose her words wisely.

"I love you." He opened his mouth, but she said, "Hush. I'm the dispatcher. I do the talking." She could feel her fingers trembling in his, and his lips—the lips she wanted to kiss, over and over—curved into a smile. "I think I've always loved you. Since the day you cried at my father's funeral. I think I knew that day I couldn't love another man in the fire services. Since that day, I knew I couldn't have you. And that's why no one I've ever dated has worked out."

Coin's voice was rough. "Why?"

"Because not one of them was you."

"Darlin'."

"I'm so sorry."

He laughed, a rusty noise, and no sound had ever made Lexie's heart more glad. "I'm not. I'd take a couple more bullets just to hear you say you love me again."

She lowered her mouth to his ear and whispered it to him. "I love you, I love you, I love you." Then she moved her lips to his, and before she kissed him, she said it again, in a different way, in a way she knew he'd understand.

"Always."

EPILOGUE

"**Y**ou have to see this."

Lexie groaned and buried her face in her pillow. "S'early. Too early."

"No, you have to get up."

She rolled to her side and looked at Coin through tangled eyelashes. "You keep me up all night and this is what I get?" She twisted to look at the clock on the bedside table. "At five forty-five in the freaking morning?"

"Just get up."

"I'm going to kill you."

"I think you gave it your best shot last night, darlin'. I'm proving pretty hardy, I think."

"Hardy as a weed. As Bermuda grass," she grumbled, but she took the hand he offered as he led her out of the bedroom and onto the deck.

Outside, scarlet warred with crimson as the sunrise split the sky right down to the bright blue water. Huge clouds loomed, banked with blue darkness, the red dawn spilling gloriously behind them. A storm was on the way to the island and far out on the purple horizon, Lexie could see a water spout dance.

Lexie clutched the bamboo railing. "It looks like ..."

"Like the whole sky is on fire." Coin grinned and turned his face to the dawn.

"Let's move here," said Lexie, staring at how the palms bowed and swayed in the tropical wind that was still warm even though it was getting stronger. The air smelled of plumeria and salt.

"I don't have the equipment to fight this kind of fire. I don't think anyone would hire me."

Lexie nodded in agreement. "You don't have the training, I guess."

"No training to fight sky fire, no." Coin wrapped his arm around Lexie's waist and pulled her against him. "I have other skills."

"That you do. Like having girls pay your way to Bora Bora."

"Only one direction," he protested. "And I'm paying our way back. And anyway, with what we're going to save by living together—"

Lexie cut him off with her laugh. "I'm teasing you, my love. Hey, what time is it at home?"

"Almost nine a.m."

"Let's call Serena."

Coin smiled and pressed a kiss against her forehead, warming her even more than the rising sun did. "Okay. Why?"

"Because that looks like a big storm coming."

"You worried about the lines going down? I think it's all satellite now, but okay ..."

"No, big guy. I need you to check off your only to-do, because I have big storm plans for that hotel bed."

"I see," said Coin. "And you call your mom. Just to check her off the list."

Lexie nodded. "She's been so much better ever since I told her to back off."

Coin said, "I think it's me. She adore me, what can I say? What about supplies? Do we have enough to ride out a typhoon? A firefighter's always prepared."

"Let's see," Lexie said, and Coin pulled her against him, hard, showing her exactly how prepared he was. "Candles. Plenty of those in the cabana. All that wine we bought last night. Pineapple, and mango, lots. Extra bubble bath. I think we're good to go."

"You still sleepy?" Coin nipped her bottom lip then soothed the bite with a kiss.

She kissed him back, and after a long moment, she said, "No. But I want to go back to bed."

"Darlin'."

It was all Lexie needed to hear.

She glanced at the fire in the sky behind him as they went back inside.

Always.

PREVIEW OF FLAME

K eep reading for a preview of the third book in The Firefighters of Darling Bay series, *Flame*.

FLAME - CHAPTER 1

THE MAN CAME at her fast from the side, out of the shadows. His fist swung toward her jaw but Samantha ducked and caught the blow on her forearm. "No!" she yelled. "Stop!"

The man wheeled, coming back at her again. He roared, driving his fists against her shoulders, slamming her back into the brick wall, knocking the wind out of her.

Samantha took almost a full second to think, to dig inside herself for what she needed. The man was taller, broader, and outweighed her by sixty pounds. He had her pinned against the wall, and she could move nothing but her right leg.

That would be enough.

She kicked her foot left, driving her heel into her assailant's shin. His response was muffled but clearly displeased.

"No!" she managed to shout again. "No!" Her foot connected again, this time higher. She might have hit his kneecap.

One last time she yelled "Stop! Someone call 911!" The

man pulled back his head, as if her voice had hurt his ears. Samantha used the moment to shove her shoulder forward, freeing her right arm from his grip. Without a pause, she raised her fist and pummeled his ear, or where his ear would have been. She propped her foot against the wall and used it to push off from. The man lurched backward, struggling to keep his grip on her upper arms.

With a jerk of her neck, Samantha head-butted him, earning a muffled, "*Ooof.*"

Both her hands finally free, Samantha flew into motion. She jabbed, punched, kicked and clawed. She was a piston, each pump a blow. She didn't stop until the man was on the ground, curled onto his side, his arms protecting his head.

She'd done it. She'd won. Samantha's heart beat heavy and fast in her ears. No matter how many times it happened, she was always frightened. That was the point. Fighting past the fear. She turned to face the group behind her.

"This is when you run. Don't waste your breath calling for help at this point—right now you're using all your energy to put as much space between you and him. Get to a well-lit space or behind a locked door. Find a phone. Find a safe group of people and ask them to call 911. I call it *Down and Out*. He goes down, you get out."

A light laugh rippled around the room, but mostly Samantha heard rapid breathing as women took in quick sips of air. The first scene was always the second-worst part of the class. The worst part, of course, was the first fight each woman took part in.

The *best* part was the first scene each woman won, but they were still quite a way from learning how to do that.

"I know. This is intense. Take a deep breath."

The participants, to a woman, looked as if they might

fall right over, especially Linda McCracken, a woman who had been considering taking the class ever since her husband died a few months before, and was observing today. She'd looked nervous just walking in the door, but now she had a sheen of perspiration at her hairline and her hands were clenched at her sides.

Samantha said, "I mean *all* of you. Each one of you. You, too, Linda. Breathe. Right now. In..." A collective inhaled breath was followed by the out-breath. "Good."

Their eyes were all on Jim Hinds. Of course. Samantha had just beaten the tar out of him and he was still lying on the ground behind her.

"Jim's an old hand at this," she reassured them. "And he's trained for years to take this kind of beating. I've only been punching him for two months, but he worked down the coast for one of my trainers for a long time. He can take a lickin', for sure. Come on, Jim, stand up and strip out of the suit. Let them see who I was actually protecting myself from."

It was always a nice moment when Jim Hinds took off the padded gear and the women saw that the terrifying assailant, the stuff of nightmares, was actually the well-built librarian without his glasses on.

"Come on, Jim." Samantha turned. He was still lying exactly where he'd fallen. "Show them what you look like under all that padding."

But in the big white suit, Jim remained still.

There was another collected gasp. Linda McCracken started to weep.

"Jim?" Samantha leaned over him. "You all right, buddy?"

A strange wheeze was the only answer she got. Samantha dropped to her knees and pulled off Jim's helmet as gently as she could. His skin was pale and sweaty. His eyes met hers and telegraphed what he needed.

Samantha said clearly to Martina Miller, standing in the front row, "Use the pay phone by the front door. Call 911."

Martina's eyes widened. "Really?"

"This isn't part of the training. 911. *Now.*"

CHAPTER 2

H ANK COULDN'T BELIEVE it.

Samantha Rowe. Again. How many times was he going to have to be thrown together with her? Not that he didn't want to be—no, wait. That was right. He *didn't* want to be.

Even Coin noticed it. "Doesn't it seem like you run into her everywhere you go, dude? What's it been, at least five times? You gonna ask her out or something?"

"No way." The truth was that he'd seen or talked to her *six* times since she'd gotten back to town. The first time had been when she'd had the car accident at the pier—he'd been so shocked to see her he'd dropped the jaws of life on his toe. Since then, he'd made up excuses to go call or text her, asking her silly questions like how long she was going to be in town, and what she thought of the acupuncture her sister practiced.

Thin excuses, all of them.

Then he'd heard she was seeing John Selzer, the used-car salesman who liked his women loud and accomplished in the flirting department, and Hank had realized that he'd fallen right back into his old pattern of crushing on Samantha Rowe, setting himself up for nothing but failure.

Yeah, he'd already spent years doing exactly that, before Samantha left town with a guy on a motorcycle, taking Hank's heart with her.

He wasn't doing *that* again.

But inside the community center, with her eyes on him, it had been all he could do not to pump Jim Hinds for information when they'd hooked him up to the 12-lead. Jim was awake by the time they got there, though his gray color made it clear he wasn't doing well. His rhythm had been far enough off that they'd packaged him for the ambulance, which had rumbled off code two, leaving Hank and Coin and Tox standing on the sidewalk in front of the center where Samantha Rowe was apparently teaching women to defend themselves.

"Yo! We're going to get pizza to take back to the station." Tox banged the engine door shut.

"No," started Hank. "I know what you're trying to—"

"Back soon," said Coin with a grin.

"You both suck," Hank growled. "Hurry it up."

Because Tox and Coin were both going in to Junior's Pizzeria, Hank was the one who, by default, had drawn the short straw and had to stay behind with the engine.

Normally it didn't bother him. He was, after all, the most junior of the crew, and it happened to him a couple of times a week. He got to put the radio on the channel he liked (country, which had the added benefit of seriously irritating Tox when he got back in the rig). He didn't mind talking to citizens as they walked by—and everyone had something to say when they passed a fire engine—even when they were actively criticizing the department. *I can't believe you're just sitting here, waiting for someone to have a fire. Hard day, son? Are my tax dollars paying you to look at your phone?*

Hank would just shrug and say, "Someone's gotta do it, sir." Because those same citizens were the ones who would expect them to arrive at their homes twenty seconds after they dialed 911, and on those days, they were nothing but grateful to see the fire engine turning down their street. Some of the guys hated taking the flak, but Hank didn't mind. His shoulders were broad enough.

But right now? Sitting in front of Samantha Rowe's self-defense class while his partners got pizza? Tox and Coin were jerks, plain and simple. It never paid to admit a weakness to anyone in the fire department, never.

And Samantha was a weakness, all right.

That moment, what was it, eight months or so ago now? When they'd pulled up in the engine, when they'd seen that car perched on the edge of the pier, smashed halfway through the railing, teetering and swaying—Hank had known that whoever was inside had to get out, and fast. If the car hit the water, it would be bad. Really bad.

But then Hank had gotten to the side window and looked inside the vehicle to see Samantha Rowe in the passenger seat—completely unconscious.

The girl who had broken his heart. The woman he'd compared all other girlfriends to—it hadn't been fair to them, of course. He knew that. But he couldn't help it. When he was dating Joanne, he'd compared her plain brown eyes to Samantha's brilliant green ones. When he and Nicole had been an item, he'd remembered Samantha's enormous, almost startling laugh, placing it next to Nicole's timid one.

He'd learned about Platonic ideals in a college class (had she been in that class too? No, probably not. If she had been, he wouldn't remember a darn thing about the subject). Samantha was his Platonic ideal of the perfect woman—confident, beautiful, smart, and funny.

And there, on that pier, she'd been an inch away from death, and he was one of the men working to save her.

In a movie, he would have been the one to cut open the door, to pull her to safety just before the car plunged to the water so far below.

In reality, he was one of a team of guys who worked fast and accurately. Tox pulled her out and Coin was the one who helped the medics lift her onto the backboard.

In a movie, her lashes would have fluttered just as she was being wheeled away. They would have locked eyes and exchanged pieces of their souls as she was loaded into the ambulance.

In reality, she didn't wake up for hours. Not until she was at the hospital, and when he went to check on her, he'd been rewarded by a super-friendly greeting. The kind one gave an old acquaintance from college, in fact. Which was exactly what he was to her. They should catch up! Have coffee sometime!

Damn it. He'd pretty much planned on never seeing her again, and now that she was in town, and he knew he was going to have to, he'd planned on just trying to stay away from her.

Instead? He'd stepped right into the friend zone. She'd grabbed him one morning at Mabel's Cafe and bought him a cruller. Bought *him* a cruller. Wouldn't even let him buy her a coffee.

If he could just get her out of his system, once, for good...

What would that be like?

How would it feel to go on a date with a nice woman he

didn't compare to Samantha? Maybe he could finally make a go of it with someone, someone he could introduce to his Gramma Maureen, the woman who'd raised him. Someone he could settle down and fall in love with, someone he could have those babies everyone else was having. Hank dreamed of kids, a passel of them, running around the house, filling it with noise and dirt and rambunctiousness.

He'd just never been able to picture anyone to have them with. Anyone that didn't look like Samantha, that was. Every girl of his dreams that he imagined had that same thick brown hair hanging to her mid-back, each one had those sparkling green eyes and that nose that slanted upward, right at the very tip. Every dream girl had her figure, too: just right, not too slim, with—let's face it—a rack that just wouldn't quit.

Three women exited the Darling Bay Community Center chattering excitedly about the drama of Jim Hinds hitting the dirt. One smiled up at him, and he smiled back, his teeth clenched. Hopefully Samantha had a lot to do inside and wouldn't come out till they'd left. She probably needed to put whatever they worked with away, and probably had to close windows and doors and set the alarm...

No such luck.

Samantha waved at him cheerfully as she came out of the building.

"Hank! I'm so glad you were on the engine that came to help Jim!" She stood at the foot of the open door and looked up at him. "Where are the other guys? Can I come up?" She started climbing the steps before he answered, leaving him to scramble backward in surprise.

"Whoa," was the only thing he could think of to say.

CHAPTER 3

"WHAT?" SHE PULLED back. The way Samantha barreled forward, Hank knew she was probably used to having to self-correct. "I'm not supposed to be up here?

Not technically, no. She wasn't. The only people allowed on board were either paid by the Darling Bay Fire Department or specially cleared for ride-alongs. If Chief Barger rolled by and looked up to see a citizen in one of his rigs? Heads would roll, and the first head spinning would be Hank's.

But instead of telling Samantha Rowe that she couldn't climb up, Hank reached a hand down to help pull her up. He felt that stupid grin cross his face, the one he always got when she was anywhere around. *Dummy.* "Come on. Watch your head there." He pointed her to the spare jumpseat. "Are you okay?"

"That was terrible! So scary!" she said, leaning forward so she could rest her elbows on her knees. For a moment, he forgot she was talking about Jim Hinds and thought she was talking about the climb up. She'd always done that to him—

confused him until he didn't know what was up or down. Her hair, that wonderful brown waterfall, fell forward and, for a moment, hid her eyes. Was she crying? Hank felt two simultaneous urges: to leap forward and wrap his arms around her and to throw himself out of the rig. No *way* was he worrying about her again. No way.

Samantha looked up at him, but instead of tears, her bright green eyes were sparkling with excitement. "That was *amazing*, what you did."

They really hadn't done much. They'd assessed Jim and strapped him to a gurney. His pulse on the 12-lead was strong enough that they didn't even go code three. "Nah."

She laughed, that sound as pretty and sweet as whatever light scent she was wearing, the scent that Coin with his dog's nose would be able to pick up as soon as he climbed back on board. "You saved a man's life."

Saving lives was what they did. And Jim hadn't been a save so much as a push to the hospital where he definitely needed to be seen. Something was wrong with the guy, but nothing immediate. "He'll be fine. He'll be home tonight, nursing those bruises that got put on him by your group of aggressive women. What were you doing to him in there?"

Samantha flapped her hand. "Ah, you know. Beatin' the tar out of him. Every girl's gotta learn how sometime."

"It looked like you were killing him."

"No, it didn't! Did you see how well he was suited up?"

"It wasn't easy to get through all that padding to get the leads on, so yeah. But did you see that bruise on his right arm?"

Samantha looked a little guilty. "It's possible that Myra Tenbottom got a little carried away with her kicking. But that just means she was *really* into it."

Hank straightened his legs. The hardest thing about

being the firefighter in the back of the rig was that it wasn't big enough to fully stretch out. Right now while the door was still open was the ideal time to do it. "So, what is it that you do in there, anyway?"

"I teach women how to defend themselves against would-be attackers."

"That's great."

Samantha looked surprised. "Really?"

"Of course."

"The reaction I've gotten in this town doesn't always go that way."

Darling Bay could be a little provincial, but... "What do you mean?"

Samantha looked out the small window as if looking for someone. "Men usually wonder out loud who it is we're going to beat up." She made air quotes around the last two words. "I always tell them that if they're that worried about it, maybe they shouldn't be around the women that train at Daring Darling."

Hank nodded. It was a good answer. "I like it. What about women?"

"I get one of two responses. Either they say how cool it sounds and how much they want their niece, sister, mother, and aunt to take it, or I get silence."

He filled in the blank in his mind. "That's what you don't want to get."

"Yeah. That means it's too late, and they should have already known what to do in the past."

"In Darling Bay?"

"Everywhere. In every town. One in five women will survive rape or attempted rape, and ninety-seven percent of rapists won't ever stay a night in jail."

"Well, heck." Hank stretched out his hands, looking at the knuckles. "I hate that so much I can't even stand it."

"Well, yeah."

"What can I do to help?"

"What?" She sounded startled.

"People have to ask you that."

"Strangely enough, no."

"How long have you been doing it?" Hank had been seeing the flyers up around town for at least the last four months—Daring Darling Defense, a silhouette of a woman standing proudly upright in front of a darkened door.

"Seventeen weeks." Samantha sounded proud. "But it's going really well."

"Until you knocked out your attacker."

Samantha barked a short laugh. "Yeah. *Crap*. He'll be back. Right?" Her eyes were worried. "Right?"

"Maybe?" Hank hated to lie, even when he should.

"But you don't think so?"

"A guy with that coloring?"

"You mean pink and white?"

"He left out of here gray. That's not a good sign for either his heart or his lungs. He might be out a while."

Samantha pulled up her legs and wrapped her arms around them. "No. I need him."

"He's your only guy?"

"I have another one, Wally, but he's so skinny that the women just toss him around like a teacup."

"Wally Atkins? Isn't he over sixty?"

She looked chagrined. "Well, it's pretty easy for the more advanced to block him."

"Block him? They'll kill him."

"I know." She sighed, blowing a breath out. A brown curl swung next to her face and Hank tried not to notice how her chest rose in her T-shirt with each breath. That rack of hers had only gotten better with time. "I need to come up with a better plan."

"I'll do it." Hank knew as soon as he said it that he wanted it. He wanted to help. To save her. Okay, to save her business. But wasn't that kind of similar? Even while his inner voice told him he was just falling into the same old pattern, he said, "I'll help. If you want me to."

"You'd train to be an attacker?"

"Yeah."

"Do you have any idea what that entails?"

"Beyond being beaten up by a bunch of angry women? No."

"First of all," she raised one finger, "you'll have to realize that it's not a bunch of angry women. It's a bunch of women appropriating their much-deserved autonomy, realizing that they don't have to rely on a man to take care of them. It's a bunch of women figuring out they're as strong as or stronger than many men, and that they can learn how to use their bodies to their fullest potential in terms of protection."

"That sounds a lot better."

"And two, you'll have to learn how to wear the suit and come at a woman." She made a stabbing motion at the bridge of her nose as if she was pushing invisible glasses back up.

"I can do that."

"Can you?"

Hank rubbed his face. He wanted to. He shouldn't want to. He should just stay out of Samantha Rowe's way. For his own sake. "Yes."

"What if I came at you right now?"

"Huh?"

"What if I tried to hit you? Would you even be able to fend me off, let alone push me to the floor or against a wall?"

The unbidden image of him pushing her against the door of the engine, his lips on hers, filled his mind.

Samantha came off her seat and launched herself at him, her arm swinging. She stopped just before her fist made contact with his cheek. Hank scrambled sideways and almost fell out of the open door of the rig. Holding on with one hand, his foot twisted on the outer step, he took a quick look around to see if anyone had seen his more-than-ungraceful lurch from the seat.

"No," said Samantha, folding herself back onto her seat.

"No, what?" Hank pretended he'd been making a move to check the radio in the front. He turned it off and back on, waiting for the power-up beeping to stop before he said, "Was that a test?"

"You failed."

"What? Because of my lightning-fast reflexes?"

"Because you didn't come at me."

"Hey, now."

"You have to be able to come at a woman. With no holds barred. You can't be afraid to hurt her."

"Um. I *would* be afraid to hurt her. I'm bigger and stronger than ninety percent of the women I saw coming out of the studio, and Greta Wagner doesn't count—she's a professional bodybuilder."

Samantha looked startled. "I *knew* she was stronger than she was letting on. But that's not what I'm talking about. What you're training them to do is to feel a man's strength, the force of someone coming at them with all their might, and then getting it done anyway. Fighting back. And winning."

"What if they don't win? How do you keep them safe so that your attacker doesn't hurt them?"

She shot him a quick, amused look. "Oh, yeah. You're going to be fun to train. Are you sure about this? You think you can handle it?"

Handle being around Samantha Rowe? For hours and hours? No way could he handle it. He didn't *want* to handle it. But he found himself nodding anyway. And if he got to help one woman feel safer as a result, he could call that a well-spent day.

"Good," she said. "Are you off-duty tomorrow?"

He nodded again, dumbly.

"Come by the center at nine?"

Hank said, "I'll be there."

Boy howdy, would he ever. And damn it, just like that, the fire was back in him when he thought of Samantha Rowe. The years he'd spent getting over her were gone up in a puff of smoke that smelled like flowery shampoo.

He didn't even want those years back. When it came right down to it, he didn't mind as much as he should. When Tox and Coin climbed back onboard, Coin flinging two pizzas onto the spare seat so recently vacated by Samantha Rowe's delicious backside, he didn't even care that they'd bought pepperoni again, instead of the sausage he preferred.

It was all good.

He was going to see Samantha Rowe tomorrow. And maybe, just maybe, get to tackle the heck out of her and not get in trouble for it.

KEEP READING!

Keep reading by grabbing *Flame* now! Just go to RachaelHerronBooks.com to get your copy!

(Psst - there are special discounts over there, too!)

ABOUT RACHAEL

Rachael Herron is the internationally bestselling author of more than twenty books, including thriller (under R.H. Herron), mainstream fiction, romance, memoir, and nonfiction about writing. She received her MFA in writing from Mills College, Oakland, and she teaches writing extension workshops at both UC Berkeley and Stanford. She's a New Zealand citizen as well as an American.

She'd *love* to hear from you! Sign up for her mailing list at RachaelHerron.com/Subscribe, then drop her a line and she'll write you back! (Seriously. She loves to hear from readers.) Plus you'll get a free short love story that will melt your heart, instantly! Or find her on social media!

instagram.com/rachaelherron

patreon.com/rachael

facebook.com/Rachael.Herron.Author

bookbub.com/authors/rachael-herron

youtube.com/@RachaelHerronWrites